NORTH NOTTINGHAMSHIRE

SHORT STORY COMPETITION
2016

First published 2016 by Bookworm of Retford
1 Spa Lane, Retford Notts. DN22 6EA
www.bookwormretford.co.uk

ISBN 978-0992785758

These six short stories are works of fiction
and are not representations of historical fact.

Copyright

All rights reserved. No part of this book may be re-printed
or reproduced in any form without prior consent
in writing from the publisher and authors.

This book is sold subject to the condition that it shall not
by way of trade or otherwise, be lent, resold or otherwise
circulated without the publisher's prior consent in any form of binding
or cover other than that in which it is published and without a similar
condition being imposed on the subsequent purchaser.

A catalogue record of this book is available from the British Library.

CONTENTS

FORWARD - CLLR. JO WHITE   5

BLOOD AND FIRE - JACQUELINE MANDY COGGON   7
ONE GOOD DEED - NICOLA HAXBY   27
PROMISED LAND - MEL E GOLD   47
BELIEF AND BETRAYAL - LESLEY MIDDLETON   77
HIS BOOTS - STEVE TAYLOR   109
PRAY FOR THEM - CLARE EVANS   129

FORWARD

CLLR JO WHITE

DEPUTY LEADER

BASSETLAW DISTRICT COUNCIL

2016

In 2014, Bassetlaw District Council undertook a Place Shaping exercise which led to the authority looking at who we are and what we do, in a very different way.

Three strong themes emerged from the place shaping initiative; themes that give North Nottinghamshire its identity and form the basis from which we will grow in the future.

In addition to 'Breathing Space' and 'Connected Values', the third theme is 'Storyscape'. Because we are, literally, a landscape rich in myths and legends, intrigue and interest. And so, the seeds were sown for our first Short Story competition.

We chose a theme for 2016, Rebels and Religion and I must admit I was pleasantly surprised how this captured the imagination of our budding authors. We had stories of knights and cavaliers, semi-autobiographies from the present day and a science fiction story from the far distant future. Thanks to everyone who took time to enter the competition.

May I take this opportunity to thank our three judges, Angela Meads of Bookworm in Retford,

Rick Brand, Chair of Bassetlaw Christian Heritage and Jonathan Brassington, Communications Manager at the council.

They have all enjoyed reading the submissions and had lively discussions on those stories that would be selected for short-listing.

Well here they are. I hope you enjoy reading them as much as we did.

Congratulations to all short listed entrants and to the three prize winners in particular.

Our Short Story Competition for 2017 is based on the theme 'Sherwood and the Dukeries' and competition details will be announced early in the year.

We look forward to repeating the success of the annual North Nottinghamshire Short Story Competition.

JACQUELINE MANDY COGGON

BLOOD AND FIRE

1ST PRIZE

Mandy Coggon has been a full-time intensive care nurse for almost thirty years. Her job involves high levels of stress and raw emotion on a daily basis. In order to unwind she likes to make the most of her precious time off and be in the company of family and friends.

She gets great pleasure from reading true life stories and acts of bravery through despair and adversity. She never fails to be amazed at how the human mind and body can recover from terrible acts of cruelty or serious illness.

She admits to carrying many stories in her head for years, often influenced by the heart-rending situations she witnesses, the diversity of her patients, their strength and courage and the amazing camaraderie and kindness of her colleagues.

Mandy never considered herself to be a writer. She felt her stories were too personal and of no interest to others but after seeing a competition flyer in a local bookshop she decided to give it a whirl.

The 'rebels and religion' theme troubled her a little and she thought it would restrict her flow of writing and the rules also stated that there had to be some reference to Bassetlaw in the story.

Being a lifelong resident of Bassetlaw, she found this part easy as the county holds many great memories for her. She has a great affinity for the local people and their down to earth honest approach.

BLOOD AND FIRE

I guess I've always had a rebellious streak – never been one for following the crowd or conformity, and like a square peg in a round hole I felt the Nottinghamshire village of Misterton was fast becoming my prison. Devoid of life, the main focus of entertainment was fishing. At least there was a choice of fast-flowing water (the River Trent) or the more sedate flow offered by the River Idle or the Chesterfield Canal. I preferred the latter and at the tender age of twelve I was beating the boys and often the men too, collecting trophies for my angling prowess. The most trouble that anyone ever encountered was being caught in a farmer's barn climbing on hay bales. Kids would 'pinch' an empty pop bottle from outside a shop door, then hand it back to the shopkeeper for a ten pence refund, and this was considered 'hard-core'. At weekends a small group of teens would frequent the local Packet Inn where we would be ushered into the back room around a large Space Invaders machine that doubled up as a table. Wearing fingerless gloves and Parkas, we would huddle around our half-pints of lager and black, making fifty pence last for two hours. Unlike the youngsters of today, we knew nothing about fashion and would be refused entry to the local social club, let alone a nightclub.

The landlord didn't particularly like us; he tolerated us. We had strict instructions to leave by the back patio doors if the police arrived, and never come back. They never did arrive, nor did anyone else for that matter. We were the only customers he had. I yearned for different surroundings, new people to talk to, new adventures, to travel, and something to learn other than how to hold a perch to prevent its fins from spiking your hand. I suppose I was a difficult child to entertain as I struggled to find enjoyment from children's television and fantasy fiction books.

If something felt too far-fetched to be credible I would lose interest immediately, preferring to read about real places and real people who had remarkable stories to tell. It did not help that I won a scholarship and was sent to the Retford County High School for Girls whilst my brothers and friends attended the village comprehensive.

School bored me, and although I had a good network of friends I would find my attention waning as I gazed obliviously out of the windows. It wasn't that I didn't want to learn: I just didn't want to learn about Home Economics, Music, Needlework, Dance, Drama, Foreign Languages, Mathematics, Literature or History. That left a rather skeletal curriculum as far as I was concerned. Where and when would I learn about people, the world, about becoming an adult, making important decisions and doing something positive with my life? I had no idea what I wanted to be, other than that I enjoyed helping others, sharing ideas and showing people how to do things. I did not want to be a homemaker, nor the hostess with the most-ess and I absolutely despised hockey.

My handwriting could easily pass as an adult's and quite frequently I would forge a letter from my mother explaining that I needed to leave the premises at lunchtime on various errands. Whilst others were made to stay within the school grounds, I would wander the canalside talking to local fisherman, watching them land a chub or a few gudgeon before heading back for afternoon classes. My route would always take me past a little chapel on Albert Road and still today I recall the words plastered four foot high on the gable end:

"For God so loved the world, that he gave his only begotten Son, that whosoever believeth in Him should not perish, but have everlasting life."

I thought about these words often and wondered what they truly meant. Was it another story that could not be substantiated? Where was the proof? Perhaps our religious education teacher could explain. She was the oldest teacher I had ever seen and I reckoned she must have been about eighty, easily. As she tried to engage us with tales of women turning to salt, I switched off again and began drawing on my desk – adding to the years of graffiti already ingrained in the lid. In the background she began talking about prostitutes and their sexual immoralities. A few muffled giggles emanated from the class. 'Miss Oakley is a prostitute' I scrawled into the woodwork, much to the amusement of my classmates. It was a new word for me and at the age of twelve I was besieged with the vulgarities of life, things that I did not know existed.

After the bell rang we filed out of the classroom, the Bridgets, Veronicas, Marys, and Elizabeths, but not the Mandys. There was only one Mandy, the girl who somehow did not seem to fit in – me. Miss Oakley blocked my exit with her arm and asked me stay behind. A tiny lady of less than five foot tall, she was a formidable character and I was about to discover her wrath. I felt sick with fear, realising that she had seen me deface the desk, and I knew that my parents would be informed of my actions. Miss Oakley instructed me to wait in the corner facing the wall. I expected her to return with the head mistress herself, but she was back in a few minutes with a bucket of water and a scrubbing brush. "Clean that scrawl from your desk," she instructed as she began stacking chairs up and closing the windows.

"Thank goodness we do not have a telephone" was the main thought in my mind as I began scrubbing away at the desk. I tried to hatch a plan of how I could intercept the inevitable letter home in a few days' time from the head mistress. Perhaps I could get home first, especially if I could persuade Mum to stop off on her way home to renew my library books. It then occurred to me that I had missed my bus back to the village, and sooner or later my parents would wonder where I was. Tears began to stream down my face: I was surely in trouble now. I swallowed in anticipation of what was coming next as Miss Oakley pulled up a chair beside me. She saw my eyes welling up and gently put her arm across my shoulders, pulling me towards her. I wasn't used to physical contact and it felt totally alien to me. A surge of emotions streamed through my body and my tears became uncontrollable sobs. I couldn't explain the reaction that her simple gesture had evoked. She explained to me about my actions, how they had upset her but how she would forgive me, just as God forgave the prostitutes for their immoral sins. "Everyone makes mistakes," she explained, "but the important thing is that we ask God for forgiveness, refrain from making the same mistakes again, and learn from our experiences." After handing me a tissue from up her sleeve, she walked me to her car and said she was taking me home.

I had never felt comfortable with women drivers, possibly because my own mother didn't learn to drive until she was in her late thirties and every journey felt like a white-knuckle ride! In those days with no rear seat belts it was a miracle that we all survived to adulthood. Miss Oakley clambered onto her cushions and could only just see above the steering wheel. It was an experience to say the least. Contrary to what I expected, she handled the car very well and did some very impressive overtaking. Another driver pulled out suddenly in front of her, and, unlike my father, she refrained from using expletives and managed to stop without colliding. That'll be the 'forgiveness', I thought to myself. She dropped me off by the village shop so as not to cause concern from my parents and nobody was any wiser. How I admired that lady. She taught me a lot that day, but not in her lesson. She taught me respect and showed me a compassion and selflessness that I had not known.

Several years later, still unsure of a career pathway, a teacher suggested I took a voluntary 'nursing' placement at a local long-stay geriatric hospital, and how bitter-sweet that turned out to be! I knew I had found something that I enjoyed, and I became lost in another world as I marvelled at the tales that the old folk used to tell me. Sat motionless in their chairs arranged in a circle, it seemed like they were literally waiting for the firing squad to end their miserable existence.

The formidable matron, whom I shall call Sister Springer, was everything that I hoped nursing would not be. She never referred to me by name. It was always 'canary' or 'daffodil girl', after the rather unfortunate lemon uniform that I had been issued with. She would bellow down the ward, "Canary, what on God's earth are you doing? Get here now and make yourself useful!" She would push me into a cleaning cupboard or the sluice if I was lucky – with the tiniest pair of nail scissors and a huge box of incontinence sheets. (Incidentally, these were about half an inch thick and came in boxes of 100). "These want cutting in half so that they will fit into wheelchairs," she barked. The moment she left the ward, I would drag the box into the day room and continue the arduous task amongst the company of the patients. With sore knuckles and blisters to my fingers, I struggled to pour their tea, but was never happier than when I was chatting with these lovely people, asking about their families and what had brought them to be here in this ward today.

If only I knew then what I know now, I would have challenged her prehistoric ideals and taken issue with the fact that patients should not be sat on their bottoms for hours on end, let alone with soggy wet pads to macerate their pressure areas further. The rebel in me emerged once more and rather than deliver a beaker of lukewarm 'milky-tea-two-sugars' to everyone as instructed, I decided to 'spice it up' a little. I had noticed the drinks trolley in the corner and wondered if the contents would go out of date before anyone ever had a tipple. I checked with Jenny the auxiliary nurse, who assured me they were for the patients but Sister Springer was adamant that nobody in her charge would ever touch a drop. She would tell the nurses that drink was the root of all evil and that God would punish those who over-indulged in alcoholic merriment.

Within half an hour or so everyone had a glass of their favourite tipple, I had seated the card school around a small table, released the dominoes from captivity and made a group of ladies quite giddy with a promise of Bingo. If Sister had a problem with the alcohol, she would have had a melt-down with the gambling. Luckily, no money changed hands! In between calling the numbers and checking the cards I still found time to create a few hairstyles, apply some nail polish and give a mini pedicure. These people had lived amongst each other for weeks, some even months, yet being positioned in their chairs so far apart from each other they barely even exchanged pleasantries any more. Those facing the window had been forced into sleep when the afternoon sun glared down, and those with their backs to the window had not seen a tree or a bird for an eternity. From that day onwards the dayroom was duly rearranged, and I actually toyed with the idea of changing my studies to Interior Design!

It was always late when I left and ran for my bus some mile and a half away. Being a village girl, I knew nothing of the town Retford, its districts and roads leading in and out. I figured it was best that I caught the bus from the terminus in case I happened to get on the wrong one and ended up in another county. Those long bus rides home gave me time to think, and yes, nursing would be an opportunity to express myself, to truly understand people and help them. I would be doing something worthwhile and could finally break out of the village. I had my reservations, though, not least the fact that I was terrified of death and giving injections. It would be ideal if I could make everyone better simply by offering them a willing ear and a gin and tonic.

And so it was that a year later I started life as a student nurse, living and working in the Victoria Hospital, Worksop – affectionately known to us as the Old Vic. My Ward Sister was not too dissimilar to Sister Springer in her ways and rituals. All pillow case openings on her ward had to face away from the door and all sheets above the counterpanes had to measure twelve inches exactly when turned over. She would not allow any nurse to be seen 'doing nothing', and whenever she passed I would busy myself in a cupboard or at least check the expiry dates of all the drugs in the trolley for the umpteenth time. There the similarity ends. She was a very popular lady who drove a little two-seater sports car and was always tanned and perfectly made up. She wore a necklace, earrings, a dainty bracelet and always court shoes with heels to give her 'a bit of height', as she would say. In today's nursing world, the Infection Control and Health and Safety brigade would certainly have something to say!

She was the patients' advocate in every sense of the word and no matter what people might have supposed by her appearance, she was a fantastic role model for me. I liked the rebellious side to her – the fact that she could express her individuality without it compromising her ability to do her job. Beneath the painted nails, pillar-box-red lipstick, frilly cap and sleeve cuffs, there was a compassionate side. She actually cared for her charges. She even allowed the patients to have a nightcap and there was always plenty of brandy and whisky locked in the controlled drugs cupboard for those who had trouble sleeping. She would actually listen to people and was not afraid to confront even the most terrifying consultants if she felt that they were not acting in the patients' best interests. If she could flout the uniform policy I fancied that I might defy a few rules too, and took to wearing a 'Robertsons' jam golly brooch in the form of a nurse, and often dyed my hair a different colour. I remember once being called into the office for having green-tinged hair. Sister could do nothing but laugh when I innocently explained that it should have been black. Pulling the box from my bag I showed her the colour name: 'midnight-sky'. "Perhaps if you lived near the Northern Lights it might well have been," she howled.

Within days on the ward I encountered the moment I was most dreading. Hearing a loud buzzing noise, I dropped the false teeth I was cleaning and ran to see what was happening. Staff Nurse was dragging a trolley of equipment through the side room door whilst the doctor could be seen entering the ward, running towards the commotion with his white coat flapping behind him. I could never have prepared myself for what I saw next. "Come inside," called the doctor. "It's essential that you get the experience."

There in the corner of the room was Ethel, the lady who only moments ago had asked me to clean her dentures. She was lying on the floor and it looked as though she had fallen, crooking her neck and twisting her body into an awkward position. Her nightdress had been ripped from the bottom seam upwards, displaying her soiled pants and neat abdominal wound dressing. Her heavy breasts hung exposed at either side of her chest and her mouth gaped open as her toothless mouth failed to close. The doctor was applying some gel pads to her skin before pushing the paddles of the defibrillator into her chest to obtain a trace of her heart rhythm. Staff Nurse was calling for an oxygen cylinder whilst simultaneously shouting that there was 'no pulse'. Within a matter of a few minutes Ethel was purged with electricity over eight times as the doctor declared she was in 'VF', her body jerking violently with each press of his thumbs. She was given oxygen via a mask over her face and countless injections of drugs into her intravenous cannula. She had chest massage, which I swore broke at least one rib, and a medical student added to her bruises in his attempt to obtain vital blood specimens.

It was all over so quickly. Ethel was dead. Lying there surrounded by equipment. The indignity of it all, the exposure, the horror – that sight has been with me ever since. I don't blame my colleagues for the way in which she died: they did all that they could to help her; but nothing can or ever will prepare me for the ways in which some people make the transition from life into death.

As children in the village Sunday School we were taught that Jesus takes people to be 'sunbeams' when their time is up, and that from then onwards they play happily in Heaven, skipping across clouds and jumping through rainbows. I always struggled to understand when the grown-ups would say that the 'good ones' always go first. If being good was rewarded with an early death, what was the point of being good at all? I wasn't naïve enough to still believe this but felt that religion had somewhat let me down and all those lessons at Sunday School had been fruitless. Was this really the end for Ethel? Would she meet her husband again on the other side? Would there be anything good at all in this for Ethel? My gut instinct told me not. Later, when we had made her presentable for her family to say their final goodbyes, they were accompanied by a priest, who gave Ethel the last rites. I wasn't sure what the priest thought of us. I wondered if he considered us to be incompetent in our jobs, hence the need for him to come and ease the distress we had caused to her family.

Ethel stayed imprinted in my mind for days. Every time I closed my eyes I could see her and each time her eyes were boring a hole in the ceiling, terrified and alone. How I wished I could have done something more, even had her teeth cleaned and back in her mouth before she collapsed – anything. I felt as though I wasn't perhaps cut out for nursing after all. I spent fewer nights alone in my flat, preferring to drive back to Misterton between shifts, back to the bosom of the village and the sleepy life that gave me security and safety, if not boredom. I confided in Dad and told him of my worries, the fear of witnessing death again and the fear of not being able to prevent it. Would I be haunted by people I could not save? Would Jesus give me a 'black mark'?

"You don't want to worry about them that are dead," he said. "They cannot hurt you. Just make sure you have a clear conscience and do everything that is asked of you. It's them buggers living that you need to watch out for!" he said, and I remember his words as though he spoke them only yesterday. The next day I drove back to work with a renewed enthusiasm. If only my Austin Mini had a fifth gear it would have flown up the B6045 from Blyth. It was a fantastic day and I felt good to be alive. Christmas was drawing near and although I had never really been a fan of Christmas I was excited at the first prospect of spending Christmas at work.

The ward was quieter than normal as most patients were discharged home for the Christmas period if their condition allowed. I was able to spend more time talking to patients and got to know George quite well. George was a frail, grey-haired old man, a little wiry round the edges, not too unlike an Airedale terrier. He reminded me of a salty sea-dog- type character and would not have looked out of place sat on a quayside mending fishing nets. He had been diagnosed with bowel cancer and was due to have his colostomy operation tomorrow, on Christmas Eve of all days. He told me all about Big Issue sellers and how he himself had been living on the streets during his younger years and relied on the generosity of others to help him get by. He talked about a patient whom he had recognised on the ward, who had been brought in one night battered and unkempt and smelling heavily of alcohol. He had overheard a young medical student making derogatory comments about the patient, and said that he hoped I would not become judgemental during my career. He had made many friends whilst homeless and some of them had been successful businessmen before succumbing to various vices that brought about their downfall. On many occasions George had been tempted by drugs and alcohol, but it was stress that brought about the breakdown of his marriage and mental wellbeing.

It was during his time on the streets that he found help and comfort in the Salvation Army. He went on to become one of their soldiers and on many occasions was honoured to play the trumpet in their marching band. He proudly wore their metal badge on his dressing gown and explained to me that the motto 'blood and fire' represented the blood of Christ and the fire of the Holy Spirit. In return, I explained to George how my Robertsons Golly- nurse brooch signified my student diet of bread and jam, and the fact that I had collected about twenty tokens to get it! He joked that he had eaten more, especially during the war years, and so considering he was a more deserving owner I gave him my Golly brooch. We laughed and shared many more similar moments. Although he had found work, and managed to get himself a little flat, more often than not he would prefer to be outdoors and was always keen to help those less fortunate than himself. He was a truly selfless man and he taught me things about God that Sunday School never did. He was able to apply his beliefs to real-life situations and his stories of survival through adversity were far more credible than the ones I had heard as a child. I guess our chats helped George get through the long days without any visitors, enabling him to start coming to terms with his diagnosis of bowel cancer and impending surgery.

So as not to offend Sister, I would counterbalance my chats with vigorous episodes of cleaning. I would scrub the metal bedpans clean until they shone, before volunteering to do the 'flower round' at the end of the shift. It was a ritual that we had to do: removing all flowers from bedside tables before the patients went to sleep in case their beautiful blooms dared to consume too much precious oxygen during the night. Occasionally we would get the labels mixed up and some poor dear would end up with wilting garage flowers the next day instead of her lavish Marks and Spencers bouquet.

The ends of the wards were quite eerie places to be in the dark, cluttered with broken equipment, old crutches, commodes and dusty boxes of files and books. Sometimes the nurses would clear a small space to make a smoking 'den' and during their breaks they would crouch amongst the urinals and cleaners buckets to partake of a few quick puffs of a cigarette. In the middle of each ward at the rear was a metal chute down which the nurses would throw the dirty linen bags. A lorry would visit the hospital each day and take the bags to the laundry, miles away in a neighbouring town. Despite having a rubber flap over the entrance to the chute, it would always be draughty around the entrance and I would run past it quickly for fear of a creature in the chute wanting to drag me in.

It was during one of these late night bedpan-cleaning sessions that I was disturbed by a strange shadow at the entrance to the sluice. I turned sharply and was relieved to see George, who was supposedly sleeping in the four-bedded bay behind me. "Are you after a ciggie, George?" I asked. "Because I don't smoke, unfortunately."

"Nor do I," he exclaimed, and in a whispered voice he ushered me into the darkness. We almost fell backwards over some linen bags, so I hurled them down the chute and patted the top of an upturned bucket for him to sit on. He told me, "I've put some pillows under my covers, lass, so that they think I'm asleep. I've thought about this long and hard and you see I don't want no operation. My time has come and I can cope with that. I'm going now and I don't want you to breathe a word. I'll be fine, just keep it a secret and take care of your'sen, lass," he said. He proceeded to make his way to the linen chute and before I could grasp hold of the situation, or his arm for that matter, his legs were already in the chute. He pressed an object into my palm and tightened my fingers around the object. It's just that there's one last thing I want to do, you see…"

Then in an instant he was gone. I peered down the chute into total darkness. "George?" I called, but there was no reply.

Sister was advancing down the ward towards me at a rate of forty knots. "Have you finished here?" she called, before turning into the four-bedded bay. My heart missed a beat and any second now I knew that she would discover George had vanished. There would be no way she would allow a patient to sleep under the covers, curled up in a messy heap; she preferred them to sleep like regimental soldiers without any creases in the counterpanes. My jaw was gaping wide as I struggled to find the words to explain what had just happened. I never got the chance. "I don't know, just look at the state of that bed!" she tutted as she turned out the lights. "Goodnight, gentlemen," she said, before addressing me again. "Now off you trot. It's not every day you get to go home early, so make the most of it," she said, patting me on the shoulder and ushering me to the changing rooms. The night staff were already there and one of the auxiliaries began collecting the flowers in. I think I floated across the car park that evening to the nurses' accommodation, as I do not recall my feet actually moving or touching the ground. My hand was white, having being clasped tightly around an object for the last ten minutes. I gently uncurled my fingers to reveal the object: George's Salvation Army badge.

I had done a terrible thing. I had not tried to stop George leaving, nor had I raised the alarm and let Sister know. My career would come crashing down around me and I would bring shame to the profession and my family. I just had to go and look for George and bring him back to the ward. Gripped with fear I crept quietly across the car park to the linen trailer and carefully dragged a bench over so that I could climb on it and peer inside the container. The black, velvety sky cast shadows in the trailer and all I could decipher were different shades of black. "George, are you there?" I called in a hushed voice. No reply. My eyes strained to take in the surroundings, but all I could see was blackness.

Maybe he had clambered out of the trailer and collapsed in the churchyard? I had only ever seen one dead body and I was not mentally equipped to go looking for another one in the middle of a cold December night, let alone in a graveyard. I looked across the road at the Priory Church, its Norman twin towers topped with miniature spires, illuminated by the floodlights below. Was George out there somewhere? I returned to my flat and tossed and turned all night, dreading the next day at work. Would I be greeted by Sister, the Senior Nursing Officer and the police, all eager to interrogate me prior to my dismissal? I sat on my bed unable to sleep at all. The words of Miss Oakley, my former teacher, came flooding right back to me: "If God did not forgive sinners, Heaven would be empty". I prayed like I had never prayed before. I prayed for George's safety and for him to be somewhere warm and comfortable. I prayed for forgiveness in the hope that I could keep my job and show that I was a good person and that ultimately I could make it to the 'Big House' one day and meet The Man himself. The day shift came so quickly despite the fact that I had so much more praying to do.

Darkness still prevailed as I crossed the car park and passed the linen trailer. I heard a scratching noise and in terror I turned to see a cat rummaging around the waste bins. We were the only signs of life. The Old Vic was still asleep and the morning was yet to break. Sister was waiting to give us the daily handover in her office, perfectly made up as usual, and despite being almost thirty years my senior she looked remarkably young and refreshed. I struggled to make eye contact with anyone, staring hopelessly at the floor. Sister made a cough to gain our attention. This was the moment, the moment I would be disgraced and brought to justice. "Unfortunately, everyone, George went missing last night..." she began. "He absconded some time during the night but left a note in his bed, along with some pillows to disguise his absence. He says he has changed his mind about the operation and wants to simply take his chances. He also wants to thank everyone for what they have done, so please don't blame yourselves, staff. He was free to leave at any time and he was in sound mind to make that decision. The night staff alerted the police in case they came across a gentleman wandering around in the cold wearing only pyjamas but unfortunately there have been no sightings of him. Now, try not to worry about George and I'll keep you informed if I hear anything." She then proceeded to give the handover report of all the other patients, but I heard none of it.

Working alongside an auxiliary nurse, I made a start on the bed-bathing and bed-making. Everyone had their own ideas as to what might have happened to George and he was the topic of conversation throughout the shift. Some thought he must have gone to a friend's house and others thought he could have reverted to living on the streets. All I knew was that he could be out there somewhere, dying or even dead. The winter sun slowly emerged, and with it the sound of traffic and passers-by busying themselves for Christmas.

I enjoy giving gifts to people at Christmas and watching their reactions to what I have selected or made for them, but I absolutely despise the physicalities of Christmas shopping. I hate the crowds, the pushing and shoving, and the queues, but most of all I hate the irritating music that our ears are assaulted with in every single shop. After numerous verses of Frosty the Snowman and Rudolph the Red-Nosed Reindeer, I am usually beaten and resign myself to going home empty-handed.

I was thankful to be inside the shelter of the hospital, away from the hustle and bustle, and knew that I would not have to queue for twenty minutes in order to get my morning cup of tea. The hospital tea bar was unusually quiet and I had time to reflect again. I could not forgive myself if George was dead or injured in the trailer, so how could God forgive me? I could not comprehend that this Almighty Being would direct an ounce of kindness in my direction. Yet George was the epitome of kindness. He deserved more. "Cancel that toastie," I called to the tea lady, and legged it back downstairs and out through the rear entrance of Casualty. I just had to check the trailer again. It was not the icy cold air that brought me to a sudden halt. Parked up close to the exit doors was an ambulance with its rear doors slightly ajar. Inside, I could vividly make out a pair of hospital issue pyjamas and a navy blue dressing gown. There laid lifeless on the stretcher was an elderly man, his wiry grey hair hanging windswept to one side. His large nostrils facing me were flared and black. I could make out parts of his yellow waxy face staring upwards and was startled by how cold he looked. His legs were hunched up towards his abdomen and his arms twisted across his body as though comforting an ache. George.

I felt the bile rise up from my stomach and a sense of nausea swept over me. I reached for the wall to steady myself. Suddenly, a doctor carrying a stethoscope and some papers entered the ambulance, followed by a nurse. "It's a B.I.D that needs certifying," she said, closing the door behind them. Brought In Dead. BID was the acronym she used – so succinct and final. I thought about the conversations we had had. This man who knew so much about the world we lived in, all the experience and knowledge that he had, the kindness and respect he shared for fellow human beings, what he had taught me… had it all amounted to this? B.I.D?

Conscious of the time, I regained my composure and went back to work. Very soon the news of a man being brought into casualty wearing only hospital pyjamas reached the ward. The senior nurses felt that he might have lived another eighteen to twenty-four months had he undergone the surgery. The junior doctor felt that he was lucky to last the night considering the weather outside and the 'state of his lungs'. I remembered that George did not smoke but made no contribution to the discussion. If only I had spoken up. Thankfully they mistook my silence for my lack of clinical judgement.

The few patients who remained on the ward were happily chatting to visitors whilst Sister did her rounds and wished them all a very merry Christmas, inviting them all to come at any time tomorrow and not just at visiting hours. Not wanting to take part in any festivities, I made myself especially busy by sterilizing all the Nelson Inhalers and cleaning the commodes. "It's a perfect opportunity," I told Sister. "We never normally have time to do these things."

Everyone was jolly and exchanging hugs and kisses as the shift drew to a close. I took a moment to look at the huge fir tree, almost touching the high ceiling. It looked bare and lonely, out of place almost like a bystander. It was sparsely decorated with what few baubles we had, a couple of metres of tinsel and a homemade star. It was a beautiful tree and would have looked so much nicer on the edge of a forest somewhere, with the sunlight caressing its branches. George had also admired the tree and on several occasions I had watched him staring at it, wondering what he was thinking. "A penny for them?" I had asked him only the other day. He responded by explaining to me the significance of the tree. The fact that it was evergreen represented Jesus and eternal life. Underneath the tree Sister had arranged the presents. It was traditional for the staff to wrap presents for each patient to open on Christmas Day, usually toiletries or small purses, bought with charitable funds. There was a present for George. I felt a tear welling in my eye and seized the opportunity to slip away quickly without any fuss. Whilst the staff were excitedly returning to their families and busy Christmas festivities, I was going home to an empty flat. I didn't mind. I needed to be alone and to think. The last twenty four hours had been quite eventful and I had to re-evaluate the way I looked at life. Christmas was only a few hours away. I had prayed for forgiveness, but felt my efforts were somewhat lacking. Sitting on the edge of my bed, staring once again at the familiar sight of The Priory Church, the answer suddenly came to me. I had never appreciated the true meaning of Christmas and if I was to be forgiven, I had some work to do. I would go to Midnight Mass and listen to what was said. I would try my very hardest to make sense of things and decide whether or not I could live with my secret.

The church was not how I expected it to be. Rather than its being gloomy and cold as its exterior suggested, it was quite the opposite. A golden warm glow flooded through the nave and a smell of spices and freshly cut flowers drifted through the air. As I took my seat in one of the pews I was offered a small glass of mulled wine.

"Why did He come?" began the priest. "Why did God send His son into this cruel world, a world where people would fight against each other and commit sins? I am sure we have all sinned at some time in our lives, perhaps even today." I felt the sermon was personally directed at me and at any minute a huge finger would appear from the roof and point me out for all to see. "The only way to make sense of this life is through Jesus. If we believe that Jesus died for our sins, we can ask Him to enter our hearts and to forgive us," he continued. It was a similar message to the one that Miss Oakley gave me back at school. I hadn't really accepted that others shared this point of view and here was a whole church full of people sharing the same concept and faith. They appeared to be at peace with themselves, content in their lives, happy, and above all they appeared to be normal. I was about to head home after the first hymn (to which I lip-synched – singing was never my strong point) when I heard the band. Marching down the aisle of the church playing O Come All Ye Faithful came the Salvation Army Band. How fitting. Here I was thinking about George; he would have loved this. The beautiful crisp clear tones of the trumpet ricocheted around the church, filling my heart with joy. As the band passed by and approached the altar, its members turned to face the congregation. I felt in my pocket and pulled out the badge that George had given me. I looked to see if I could see them wearing the same badges, and indeed they were – all but one. My eyes tracked to the one red jacket without the traditional crested badge – the trumpet player. He was an elderly, grey-haired man with his cap pulled low over his eyes. I noticed it was on the opposite lapel to everyone else's badge. A bit of a rebel, I thought to myself, rather like myself! Then I noticed that it wasn't the badge of blood and fire. It was the Robertsons Jam Golly nurse.

I could not contain the enormous smile that erupted from my face. This was going to be a great Christmas after all.

NICOLA HAXBY

ONE GOOD DEED
2ND PRIZE

Nicola Haxby is a local resident who has family ties to Retford spanning back over six generations.

Her story, One Good Deed, was inspired by stories she was told as a child and whilst the storyline is purely fictitious it surrounds real events which happened in her home town.

Whilst she is accustomed to writing full length novels, she thoroughly enjoyed writing this short story and hopes it is a fitting tribute to the many who lost loved ones during the diphtheria outbreak and to St Alban's church.

This story is dedicated to all the lives lost in the Second World War and to the many children who tragically lost their lives during the diphtheria outbreak which swept throughout England between 1935 – 1938. In addition, the story also serves as a memory to St Alban's church in Retford.

ONE GOOD DEED

It was a cold, crisp morning as Reverend George sat in quiet contemplation. The spring sunshine bathed the stained glass of the church, illuminating the halos of the angels and casting strobes of red, green, gold and blue onto the stone carved pulpit and dark oak pews. The Reverend coughed and wheezed, each gasp of air taking a little more of his already depleted energy till he managed to compose himself again. His eyes streamed as he retrieved a handkerchief from up his sleeve to dry his heavily lined cheeks before focusing on the large, brass cross at the altar. As his breathing steadied he became aware of the smell of brass polish carried upon the unique aroma of the church. Weddings, christenings, funerals, along with emotions of hope, despair, tears of happiness and tears of sadness alike, all blended in perfect harmony with the wood and candles giving him a sense of peace and tranquility.

A shiver ran through the Reverend's aged bones and he pulled the blanket a little tighter around his thin, frail legs. To his left was placed a small, carved wooden box and he ran his hand over its lid till he reached the clasp, before pausing. Its contents could have cost him everything, including his freedom – at worst, his life. Resting his hand on the box, he observed the thinness of his skin, now clearly revealing the bones of each finger, and he hoped time would help people to understand the decisions he had made. Reverend George frowned slightly as his mind took him back, pulling his gaze from the box and over to the seat on his right side. To many it was nothing more than a space on a pew and indeed many had sat there before and since, but to the Reverend it was far more. The carving was barely visible these days: years of polish had camouflaged its obviousness. All that remained was the shallow indentation of the initials – A.W. As he ran the tip of his finger along them, the young cherub-like face of Albert Worthington appeared clearly in his mind, triggering his memory that had haunted him for over sixty years.

It had been after a Sunday morning service back in 1937 when the newly appointed Reverend had first encountered Mabel Worthington. A strict and God-fearing woman, she sat rigidly upright throughout the service, rising on cue to sing the hymns she knew by heart. Beside her sat her two remaining children: Albert and his younger brother, David. The Reverend admired her strength. Despite Mabel's formidable exterior, enduring the loss of three children to the diphtheria outbreak which raged through the small town of Retford had only served to solidify her faith, never missing the Sunday morning or Evensong services. However, on this occasion, the Reverend noticed Mabel becoming increasingly agitated as the service drew to a close, and, while the congregation filtered away, she remained seated with her two boys, making no attempt to leave. The Reverend bade farewell to the last of the congregation at the door before making his way back down the aisle to where Mabel and her two young sons were still sitting. As he got closer, he noticed the elder boy, Albert, visibly sobbing.

Slightly taken aback by the boy's distress and the expression of sheer rage on Mabel's face, the Reverend tentatively asked if she needed assistance. Young Albert pleaded repeated apologies and begged for his mother's silence as he desperately tugged at the sleeve of her coat, but Mabel insisted he tell the Reverend what he had done, and sharply pulled the boy up to stand. The Reverend looked puzzled at first, his misdemeanor not initially apparent. Only when Mabel pointed to where Albert had been sitting did it become clear what the boy had done. There, freshly carved on the seat, were Albert's initials. Reverend George gave a forgiving smile as, from the expression on Mabel's face, he had expected far worse. Being of a kindly and humorous disposition, he immediately attempted to trivialise and calm the situation. The boy had only just seen his seventh birthday and the loss of his two older sisters and brother had clearly affected him, as the behaviour was very out of character. But despite his reassurances that it was nothing a little French polish would not fix, Mabel insisted the act was blasphemy and nothing short of holy desecration. Ignoring Reverend George's words, she ordered the boy to perform tasks for the church to show his repentance to God, leaving no further room for discussion.

Every day the following week, Albert arrived at the church as soon as he had finished his school day, helping to polish the brasses, sweeping the floor and tidying the hymn books. He was an endearing child with clean, blonde, slightly wavy hair and large blue eyes, and the Reverend took time between his duties to talk to the boy carefully so as not to discredit his mother's teachings. Having the innocent child filled with shame over a small error of judgement seemed wrong to Reverend George, especially given what he had been through, so he made sure to tell young Albert how God forgives all our sins – even his carving on the pew.

By Friday, the church had never looked so pristine. The brasses shone, the kneelers were all tucked neatly underneath the pews, and Albert had even brought some flowers from his mother's garden and placed them in a vase by the altar. He was clearly accustomed to chores and had needed little supervision throughout the week. In fact, Albert had performed his tasks quite chirpily as if he enjoyed being there, despite his looking rather pale the last couple of days. As a reward, Reverend George sat and shared some fresh honeycomb given to him by a member of the congregation earlier in the day, and the young boy beamed with delight as he savoured each piece before leaving to head back for home around six o'clock. As the Reverend locked the church for the evening before returning home, he wondered what tasks he could set for Albert the next day. His mother had insisted that he attend for all of Saturday but Albert had been so thorough there really were not many chores left to complete.

When bedtime arrived, Reverend George prayed he could have just one full night's sleep. He had been called out every night this week to Arlington House to give comfort to dying children and their relatives. The diphtheria outbreak had only just started when he had taken the appointment at St Alban's Church and it had placed a tremendous emotional and physical strain upon him; he had lost count of the number of children's funeral services he had performed, and in the short period of time he had been Reverend he had witnessed many tragedies. As he wearily climbed into bed, he decided that providing he was not called out to Arlington House in the night, he would spend tomorrow reading Biblical stories to Albert. If Mabel should question him, he would tell her it was for the boy's spiritual education, to appease any demands she had. As he closed his eyes for sleep to arrive, a smile played on his lips as he looked forward to the following day and seeing Albert's face light up.

The next day, Reverend George awoke slightly later than usual. His prayer for a full night's sleep had been answered, and he rubbed his face briskly before bouncing out of bed to get washed, dressed and eat breakfast before Albert arrived for his full day of chores. Despite having to rush, the Reverend managed to get over the road to the church and unlock the doors with just ten minutes to spare. Autumn had arrived and the nights were quickly drawing in. The mornings were cold and grey, but this morning for the first time since his appointment began, Reverend George had a spring in his step. He had seen so much death over the last three years, but Albert's sunny nature had given him an almost renewed positivity.

The minutes ticked by into hours and Albert still did not appear. Disappointed and slightly concerned, Reverend George ran through various scenarios as to why Albert had not arrived. Maybe he had misunderstood Mabel's instructions? He may have decided to play with some friends he met on the way; boys will be boys after all. He gazed at the books he had planned to read stories from and felt his renewed positivity ebb away slightly as he resigned himself to push the thoughts from his mind and busy himself with his daily duties.

As the congregation began to filter into the church for the Sunday morning service, Reverend George had decided he would say nothing of young Albert's absence the day before, to spare the child from the backlash of his mother. But to his surprise, the pew where Mabel usually sat with her two boys remained empty throughout the service. It was unheard-of for Mabel to miss a service and her absence perplexed him, increasing to concern when she did not arrive for Evensong. No one had mentioned anything of her absence and the Reverend decided it best not to pry. She must have good reason, and he felt it would be overstepping his boundaries to ask questions, but deep down he hoped and prayed all was well with the family. All that evening, Reverend George could not get Albert out of his mind. Thoughts of their last meeting on Friday when they shared the honeycomb and talked together filled his head. The boy had looked pale, and dark circles beneath his big blue eyes had been apparent. The thought of Albert succumbing to the same fate as his siblings tormented him. Not Albert? Surely not another child from the Worthington family? The thoughts were too painful to contemplate so the Reverend forced them out of his mind, instead keeping himself busy and dismissing them as mere foolishness.

It was early morning when Reverend George was woken by a loud banging at his front door, and it took him a few moments to realise the noise was reality and not part of his dream. Hurrying down the stairs, he tied the cord on his dressing gown on his way to the front door, briefly pausing to make sure he was decent before opening it to the caller. He knew who the caller was before having it confirmed. Only one person called at such unsociable hours, and for only one reason. Esme Dolby, nurse at Arlington House, stood on his doorstep catching her breath. She clutched her cape tightly around her chest to keep out the cold, dank autumn air, and the familiar look of distress tormented her pale face. The Reverend felt his heart sink at the realisation another child was close to death. He was only ever summonsed when they were nearing their end. Help during the illness was given by means of prayers from the isolation of the church in an attempt to confine the deadly disease. Then, as Reverend George, still shaking off the grogginess of sleep, turned back inside to get dressed, he heard the words confirming his worst fear.

Dashing as quickly as he could through the deserted streets and into the town as he made his way to the Diphtheria Hospital, Reverend George clutched his Bible. Arlington House was not far away from St Alban's and so it took him just a fraction over five minutes till he found himself at its door. Esme Dolby had gone on ahead and been watching anxiously through the front window for him to arrive, and had already opened the door to save him knocking. Without even removing his coat, Reverend George hurried up the white painted staircase, taking the steps two and three at a time till he reached the room where Albert Worthington lay fighting for his breath in a bed nearest the window. Sitting down beside the child, the Reverend took his tiny hand in his own. It was the only thing he could think of to give some comfort as he opened his Bible and prayed aloud. As he drew close to the end of the prayer, the boy's grip began to tighten and Reverend George stopped. The boy's eyes were filled with terror as he desperately fought for another breath, but to no avail. The Reverend had seen this happen too many times, each trauma no less horrifying than another. He watched helplessly as the Strangling Angel of Children claimed Albert for her own, but as his eyes rolled back in defeat Reverend George heard the boy whisper his final words, 'God's still angry with me', before his tiny hand released its grip.

Dawn was breaking when Reverend George left Arlington House to walk back home. The streets were still empty. Only Mr Reynolds extinguishing the street lights as he cycled between each one broke the stillness. Totally shattered by the experience, the Reverend felt numb as he placed one foot in front of the other without any thought to his journey, but as he grew closer and St Alban's came into view the numbness began to fade, and the image of Albert's last moments reappeared in his mind. He had never before felt so helpless, unable even to manage a few last, reassuring words to the boy. Digging deep into the pocket of his overcoat, he pulled out the keys to the church and opened its door. He stood motionless for several minutes as he stared at the large brass cross on the altar, before letting out a scream filled with anger. For the first time in his life, the Reverend questioned God and even more so, his own faith.

As the years rolled by, Reverend George spent much of his time between duties in prayer. The diphtheria outbreak had been brought under control, and there had been a couple of years where the Reverend had focused his energies in supporting the families who had been affected. Many had lost children, and keeping busy giving comfort to others helped, but try as he might the images of Albert Worthington remained etched in his mind. Sleep had become a rarity as his troubled thoughts followed him into the silence and loneliness of the night, frequently waking him to unrelenting bouts of sweating and trembling. He found solace in the company of others. The laughter and talk of working men as they enjoyed a drink after a hard day's work became a welcome distraction, and so he frequently spent his evenings in one of the town's many cosy public houses, playing dominos. He had slipped into a routine which helped him cope and function, till one day his life would once again change.

Tensions between England and Germany had escalated and despite praying for a peaceable resolution, Reverend George found himself listening to his radio to the declaration of war. Young men all over the town soon received their call-up papers. Mothers faced losing sons and husbands, children faced losing fathers and brothers and, in a matter of hours the Reverend's duties were taken away from the aftermath of the diphtheria outbreak to a different, but equally devastating, type of support. Once again the feeling of helplessness gripped him as families cried, waving handkerchiefs in the air as they bid farewell to their young men. Gas masks were issued along with ration books. Blackouts were ordered and Reverend George now found himself armed with a gun after escaping being called up due to his asthma, and instead voted into the Home Guard. Every service became filled with women and children all looking to him for comfort as they received letters informing them their loved ones would not be returning. Each week he gave services thanking the lost men for their sacrifice, reciting their names in order. The torment of Albert Worthington had now been replaced by another, freeing his thoughts of the boy during the day, only to find them returning again at night in between the raids. Night after night the haunting wail of the siren would pierce the silence, waking him from his nightmares as the enemy flew over the town heading for Sheffield or Liverpool. People huddled in the church, hardly daring to breathe as the drone of the German planes passed overhead, praying any unused bombs would not be discarded onto the town and their homes.

Months turned into years and the war felt as though it would never end. Living in darkness and surviving on rations had become a way of life, with many not being able to recall the years before its start. Already well into the fifth year of conflict, Reverend George took his turn to patrol the local streets, making sure no chinks of light were escaping from behind blackout curtains, and no glow of a cigarette could draw unwanted attention. In the beginning it had been a constant task to ensure complete darkness. But now, people had become so used to it there was rarely a need to shout out to someone to put their light out. The Reverend really did not mind taking his turn and often volunteered to take another's place to give them some rest. He had not slept well for years so the night patrol became a welcome blessing. The town was quiet and still; only the sound of his footsteps on the pavement broke the silence. He wandered, as he frequently did, past the homes on Grove Street and down the lanes into the countryside. The moon was full that evening and he could clearly see cows in the fields each side of the lane and the silhouette of the farm on top of the hill in the distance. His breath formed clouds in front of him as its warmth met the nip of the frosty air, and he wrapped his scarf over his face to avoid aggravating his asthmatic cough. He continued to stroll, listening to the nocturnal rustlings of small animals in the hedgerows, and he soon reached the crossroads where he would usually turn right. He always stopped at this point for a while.

The now deserted Diphtheria Isolation Hospital stood in darkness to his left, now nothing more than a memory. The moonlight glinted on its windows, and the vision of children's faces appeared in his mind as they stood waving to their parents beyond the fence. Among them had been David Worthington. Unaffected by the deadly disease, he had been found to be a carrier and consequently been admitted to the hospital for quarantine. Unlike his visits to Arlington House, Reverend George quite enjoyed his visits here as the children were either carriers or well on their way to making full recoveries. Reading them stories and talking with the weaker children still confined to their beds filled him with a sense of purpose and hope.

In later years, the Reverend would frequently see David around the town with his mother, Mabel. Just a small five year-old at the time he was admitted, David had spent three months away from home and every week he would appear at one of the windows to see his parents, but Mabel rarely came. Only Arnold, his father, a meek and gentle man, would always be there without fail to wave to his last remaining child. Losing four of her children had proved too much for Mabel. She was a strict and seemingly emotionless woman at the best of times, but discovering David had been the carrier of the disease had manifested a deep and bitter resentment towards the child. Now thirteen years of age, David had grown to be a quiet, self-conscious youth who, despite becoming tall and physically strong, rarely spoke because of a severe stammer. The Reverend reflected on the injustice of the situation for a while till the familiar wail of the air-raid siren wrenched him from his thoughts. German planes usually flew on missions whenever it was a clear evening, using the moonlight to search out the steel works in Sheffield, and it was not long before he could hear the sound of an engine approaching. Seeking refuge under a tree, the Reverend did his best to blend into the shadows. If he attempted to return to the church now, his movement in the moonlight could easily be spotted by the turret gunner and cause him to fire and likely drop bombs.

Reverend George stood motionless and listened as the plane got closer. He had become able to identify the type of plane just by the sound of its engines and he knew the one approaching was a Heinkel 111. Furthermore, it sounded as though it was encountering some trouble. The Reverend carefully watched from the camouflage of the tree as the plane came into view against the clear sky. Flying dangerously low above the rooftops, its engine began to misfire and splutter and the start of a fire on the left wing became apparent. He watched in horror as the crew began to drop its bombs in readiness for a crash landing. The first landed just past the railway line a few hundred yards from a house, closely followed by a second and a third thankfully hitting empty fields. A fourth exploded near to Mr Allan's farmhouse on the hill, setting a barn on fire. The Reverend held his breath. If a fifth bomb were to be released, the farmer and his family would take a direct hit. The plane banked from side to side, narrowly missing the roof of the farmhouse before disappearing from view. The only sound that followed was a loud crash and clatter of metal a few seconds later as it came down in the field beyond.

Reverend George's feet were rooted to the spot as he tried to process what he had just witnessed, and he thanked God that Mr Allan and his family had not been harmed. He began to run up the lane, fumbling to put on his gas mask, and as he got nearer, he could see the silhouettes of Mr Allan and his three sons rushing to the barn with buckets of water to extinguish the blaze. What should he do? He was the only person around, and for a moment he stopped to think. Knowing a German plane was in the field beyond the farmhouse, the Reverend continued up the lane to where it had crashed. Looking into the field over the gate he could see over a dozen small fires as the aircraft lay in pieces, nothing more than wreckage. He was certain no one could have survived such devastation. Even so, he felt it his duty as Home Guard to make sure. Climbing over the gate, he paused to check his gun. It had already been checked before he had set out on his patrol, but his nerves were causing him to doubt himself and double-check. Satisfied he had ten rounds correctly loaded, he aimed his Lee-Enfield rifle towards the wreckage as he carefully walked forward. His heart was nearly beating out of his chest as he struggled to be vigilant for any sign of movement through his mask and, in frustration, he took it off. The fires surrounding the area lit his way, and it was not long before the outline of a man lying face down on the grass came into view. Fear gripped the Reverend as he waited for the man to move, but he remained still. Reassured by his gun, he took a step forward and pushed the man over with his foot exposing the extent of his injuries, and the Reverend exhaled as he realised the man was dead. Scanning the ground before him, he saw the cockpit of the plane with the pilot's lifeless body still strapped to the seat; the turret gunner had met the same fate. Lowering his rifle, he looked back towards the farm where figures were still running back and forth with water to control the fire, but as he turned to make his way back out of the field, he heard a groan. Spinning around he raised his rifle and searched where the noise had come from. There, partly concealed by a large piece of the plane, lay a young man.

Reverend George's German was not the best; however, he knew enough to know the young man was asking for help as he stretched out his hand. What should he do? He could shoot him. For a moment the Reverend considered squeezing the trigger, but as he stepped closer with his gun aimed straight at the man, the light from a small fire lit up his face and their eyes met. Rather than seeing a face filled with anger and hate, the man had soft, almost angelic features, with large blue eyes. His hair, cropped short at the sides and back, was blonde and wavy on the top, and Reverend George froze as an image of Albert Worthington flashed into his mind. The likeness was uncanny and it had taken him by surprise. Without thinking and with no plan, he lowered his rifle and began to free the young German from the wreckage. Remarkably, he managed to stand, although even by such poor light it was obvious that he had broken his leg. Once again the Reverend froze. What now? Should he wait for the Military Police to arrive? He could hear the distant sound of voices approaching up the lane. Aggressive shouting told him an angry mob had already formed and were on their way. Soon, he could see three youths striding up the lane and he recognised them instantly to be Fred Nelson, Eric Stewart and Nobby Roberts, local trouble-makers who hated the Germans passionately. All three had lost their fathers within the first year of war being declared and, although too young to enlist, would delight in executing their own vigilante justice. Reverend George knew if he were to leave the

German or wait till the youths arrived, the young man's chances would be slim. Wrapping the man's arm around his shoulders, the Reverend quickly began helping him back down the field. He knew of a narrow gap in the hedge they could cut through, undetected. Crossing the lane and into the field which only minutes earlier had been bombed, he continued towards and over the railway track till they reached the top of Trent Street. It was only a few yards from there to his house opposite the church. The explosions had been so loud that everyone would be awake. Reverend George quickly took off his overcoat and instructed the German to put it on to hide his uniform, then removed his scarf and wrapped it around the man's face and neck. If they were lucky, the blackout would act as a cover to obscure incriminating details like his boots and blonde hair.

It was a risk – a big risk– but something spurred Reverend George to continue. Hobbling down onto Holly Road, the young German tried his best to walk as normally as possible and the Reverend noticed how hard the man was clenching his teeth in an attempt to stave off the pain. As they approached the end of the street and his house came into view, the magnitude of his actions began to sink in. He was helping the enemy. He was a traitor. The thoughts threw him into a mental panic and he pushed the young man to increase his speed. A few more yards and they reached the door of the vicarage and went inside. The blackout curtains were already in place from earlier in the evening, and so Reverend George lit a candle and lay the young man on the rug by the fire, where he could see his injuries more clearly. As well as a broken leg the man's body was black with bruising, and he cried out in pain with just the lightest of pressure. He had also gone into shock and was now visibly and uncontrollably shaking. Reverend George knew the injuries coupled with shock were not a good sign, but all he could do for him was to keep him warm and hope he made it through the night. Laying extra blankets over him and giving him a gulp of brandy for the shock, he placed an extra ration of coal on the fire and watched as the young man drifted in and out of consciousness.

Sitting in the old leather armchair, he observed the young man for most of the night. The glow of the fire flickered on his features and Reverend George realised he was not much more than a boy of around eighteen to nineteen years of age, at most. He absorbed every detail of his gentle features: his long sweeping eyelashes and the waves of his fresh blonde hair as they fell loosely on his unlined forehead – too young to be experiencing the atrocities of war. Should he be discovered, he would certainly be placed in a prisoner-of-war camp, maybe the one at Headon, where they were treated well and given a degree of freedom in exchange for work on the land. But how could he turn him over to the authorities while he was so badly injured, and what would happen to himself? The punishment for harbouring him would be viewed as an act of treason and, at the very least, cost him his position in the Church and likely a prison sentence. Then there was Fred Nelson and his gang to negotiate. He frowned as he weighed up the options, playing out different scenarios and their likely outcomes in his head before praying on the matter for clarity. Closing his burning eyes, he drifted off into a light sleep, uncertain whether the young man would survive till morning.

Reverend George awoke with a start to a loud banging at his front door. Temporarily dazed and conditioned to such noise being associated with Arlington House, he shot out of his chair and rushed to open the door, forgetting all about his guest till he slid the bolt back. Jolted back to the present day, he froze and gasped sharply as he peeped through the small glass panel to see who was calling. He hardly dared to look, half-expecting to see the Military Police standing on his pathway to take both himself and the German into custody. It was Fred Nelson with his mother, Mildred, equally unpleasant and formidable visitors. They banged again on the door. There was no escape, and so he whispered a silent prayer as he turned the handle and opened the door just enough so they could see him. As he suspected, the mob had searched the area where the plane had crashed and only discovered three bodies which had triggered a full-scale manhunt for the fourth man. Naturally, as the Reverend had been on nightly patrol at the time, he was an obvious port of call. Fred looked at the Reverend through narrowed eyes, searching his face as he delivered a story of how he had felt unwell and been in bed when the crash had happened. Lying did not come easily to the Reverend. It was against both his nature and his beliefs but a life was at stake, possibly two, if Fred and his mob got their way. After a brief conversation which felt more like an eternity, Fred and Mildred turned to walk back down the Reverend's path, but as he was about to close the door and breathe a sigh of relief, Fred spun back around and came back. Reverend George's heart was nearly pounding out of his chest and he felt sure it could be clearly heard. Fred gave him a hard, cold, hate-filled stare and without uttering a word, handed him a bag before turning and walking away.

The Reverend had never felt such a sense of relief as he closed the door and leaned against it while he caught his breath, his eyes looking upward as he once again murmured a little prayer of thanks before turning his gaze to the direction of his living room and the German. Did they suspect anything? He felt his story had been credible. Eventually, satisfied they were not returning, he left the door and made his way toward the kitchen to make a cup of much-needed tea. Placing the bag on the table, he busied himself filling the kettle, lighting the stove and placing the tea leaves in the pot in readiness for when it boiled. He watched the kettle for a while and then, remembering the old adage about a watched pot never boiling, turned his attention to the bag Fred had given him; but as he opened it up his heart almost stopped. There, inside the bag, was his gas mask, and he instantly recalled how he had taken it off the previous night and discarded it in the field. Panic gripped him like a vice as the realisation Fred and his mob knew he had been there imploded inside his stomach. He had to get the German away from here before they returned to take the law into their own hands and wreak their violent revenge. An increasing sense of paranoia washed over him and he checked the blackout curtains to ensure there was not even the slightest opening that would allow Fred to see inside. Maybe he should call the police and hand him over? After all, he had only been giving him medical assistance. He shut his eyes tightly and pinched the bridge of his nose as he realised his explanation would not be accepted as an excuse. The only option was to hide him – hide him so well he would not be found till after the war was over. But where?

The stress of the situation and the cold, damp air from the previous night had taken its toll on the Reverend, and he wheezed as he sat on the edge of his bed to put on his socks. Such was his panic; he had not even checked the young man and he could hear the kettle whistling loudly on the stove. Maybe he had not survived the night? There had been no way for him to tell if he had any internal injuries. Hurrying back downstairs, he removed the whistling kettle from the heat and poured the boiling water over the tea leaves leaving the pot to stand as he ventured back into the living room. The young man lay still in front of the fire and Reverend George quietly sat back in his chair to see if he was breathing, but to his amazement the young man turned his head and smiled at him. Once again, the striking resemblance to Albert Worthington hit the Reverend and he knew he had to do his best to help him. His English was far better than the Reverend's German and he unreservedly thanked him for saving his life, telling the Reverend his name was Otto Hepp, aged just nineteen. They talked for a short while, each one wary of the other, and Reverend George explained the situation he was in and the danger they both faced when Fred Nelson and his mob returned. Assessing Otto's injuries, he gave him another large brandy to help the pain before tearing up an old surplice and wrapping it around his broken ribs. Taking two large piece of kindling wood for splints, he placed one at each side of his leg, using the remainder of the surplice to bind them in place so the bone could set. He had decided the only safe place to hide Otto would be in his private quarters, which were located in the vestry area of the church; but with Fred Nelson onto him, it was far too risky to take him over there now, especially as it was now getting light. The only thing he could do would be to keep vigilant and wait for the cover of night to arrive again.

The Reverend spent the day watching over Otto as he drifted in and out of sleep, feeding him bread with jam and cups of tea whenever he awoke. During these times the pair talked, opening up to each other a little more as a new and fragile bond began to form between the pair. Otto handed the Reverend a photograph of a pretty young woman, his sweetheart. They had planned to marry as soon as the war was over, and as he handed the photograph back he noticed Otto's eyes had become glassy with tears. He was supposed to hate this man before him. He was a German. The enemy. But the more the men got acquainted, the more they realised they were not so different underneath.

Moving Otto was a painful task, albeit a successful one. Reverend George had waited till six o'clock. He knew enough about the local families to know that Mildred Nelson always had tea on the table at that time, and insisted her son be there before he went hawking the streets at night with the others to cause trouble. It gave him a welcome snapshot of time where they could make the short distance to the church unnoticed. He settled him as comfortably as he could, making sure he had food, water and plenty of blankets to get him through the cold February night. He could not stay with Otto for long, as he knew Fred and his mob would come back, but he assured Otto he would return in the morning. Hurrying back to his house, he rushed around each room, clearing any evidence of a second person ever having been there. He folded the blankets from the makeshift bed in front of the fire, dried and put away both of the cups and saucers on the draining board and threw the last few remnants of the shredded surplice onto the fire. No sooner had the flames taken hold than a loud, angry banging once again came at his door, causing him to jump. Although the Reverend had already rehearsed his explanation as to why his gas mask had been found in the field and was expecting Fred to return, it did not quell his anxiety and he began to wheeze as he opened his door. Sure enough, there stood Fred, this time with Eric and Nobby for back-up, and he openly invited them inside to show them he had nothing to hide. The three youths searched every corner of his modest house, much to the Reverend's outrage, but as he was outnumbered and outmatched there was little he could do. The search, along with his explanation, did little to satisfy Fred's suspicious and devious mind and instead of leaving, he demanded Reverend George open up the church. Not knowing what else to do and realising they would find Otto, he did the only thing he could think of.

Grabbing his rifle from beside the door he aimed it at Fred, ordering him and his mob to leave and chastising them for interrogating him and attempting to break the peace and sanctity of the church. None of the youths had ever seen Reverend George behave in such a way and his assertiveness caught them off guard. Raising their hands, the youths backed out of the door before turning and fleeing down the path as quickly as they could. His gamble had paid off, but he knew Fred and his friends would be watching him like hawks from now on and he would have to be extra vigilant.

The days rolled into weeks followed by months as Otto healed and gained back his strength. During the day he would sit and exchange stories with Reverend George, who kept him supplied with plenty of books to occupy his time. Otto came from a small village near the Austrian border and was the second from youngest of five siblings, much like Albert Worthington had been, and Reverend George could not help but notice the coincidence. As the bond between them grew, he realised the young man had no desire for conflict. More than anything, he wanted peace just like everyone else. Refusal to enlist, however, would have resulted in his being shot. He was a gentle, God-loving young man, certainly not the monster everyone imagined a German would be. In the evenings and during services, Otto would conceal himself quietly in the Reverend's quarters within the vestry until it was safe to come out. The arrangement worked well, but they both knew it could not go on indefinitely. Fred and the others were never far away and rumours whispered on the tongue of Mildred Nelson of his harbouring the enemy soon spread. Some members of his congregation had left in favour of other churches, whilst others looked at him with scorn. Only a few members refused to believe the accusation and backed him up against any malicious gossip.

Reverend George prayed for an end to the war and to his great joy the announcement finally came on the first of September the same year. Otto embraced the Reverend tightly and sobbed with joy and they both danced up and down the aisle in merriment at the news till they sat down in exhaustion. They puffed and panted for a while, till slowly the realisation they would have to say goodbye enveloped them. The Reverend had been Otto's only friend, a true friend who had risked his life to help him, a total stranger; a friend who, instead of seeing a German, had seen a person, a human being, a man trying to do his best in a situation not of his making or approval. Reaching into the pocket of his shirt, Otto pulled out the photograph of his sweetheart he had shown the Reverend when they had first met and placed it in his hand. He no longer had a need for it as, thanks to the Reverend, he would be reunited with her soon.

That evening, Otto sat on the back of Reverend George's bicycle as he pedalled along the quieter streets toward the police station. He knew that now the war was over, they would look after Otto and take the necessary steps to return him back home to Germany in due course. He knew Otto would not betray him. Reprisals would still be severe, and he had assured Reverend George he would drastically reduce the level of his English comprehension when they asked him probing questions. Stopping at the side of the park, the Reverend showed Otto where the police station was, pointing to the distinctive blue lantern hanging outside its front door. The men looked at each other for a moment before embracing tightly and Otto turned and walked away so the Reverend did not see the tears in his eyes. He lingered and watched Otto as he made his way towards the station, disappearing inside. He wondered if he would turn around and wave, but he never looked back.

Reverend George erupted into another explosion of coughing, barely managing to catch his breath, the white handkerchief used to cover and muffle his cough now crimson. Opening up the carved wooden box he had kept hidden for over sixty years, he pulled out an old sepia photograph of a beautiful young woman and smiled at it lovingly before placing it carefully back inside the box. As his fingers trembled, he managed to retrieve the letter. His name and address had been written in the finest handwriting, the German postmark clearly franked in the top right corner. Inside, along with a letter containing words of love and gratitude was a family photograph: men, women and children, all smiling, among them, a scientist researching a pioneering cure for cancer, another, a missionary worker dedicating his life to bring fresh water to villages in Africa. Standing beside him was his sister, who had gone on to become a midwife and who now held a new-born baby girl in her arms, completing the fifth generation of the Hepp family.

Reverend George held the photograph to his chest as overwhelming emotions surged through his body. Sunlight burst brightly through the stained glass, bouncing onto the brass cross upon the altar, causing it to glow, and Reverend George felt the presence of God. Filled with a calm he had never encountered before, he let out a long continuous sigh as his hand, still clutching the photograph, fell peacefully into his lap.

MEL E GOLD

PROMISED LAND

3RD PRIZE

Mel E Gold is an American citizen who moved to the Land of Tea and Irony thirteen years ago after marrying her British husband.

In addition to writing, Mel spends her free time singing in a local heavy metal band called 'Aonia' and is a guest backing vocalist on the latest album by Blaze Bayley (ex-Iron Maiden).

A lover of science fiction, Mel is obsessed with anything related to outer space: as a teenager, she attended Space Camp, which is one of her fondest memories.

By day, Mel is secondary school English teacher. She began writing fiction while teaching an A-level Creative Writing course, and she fell in love with creating what her editor calls "word pictures." The North Nottinghamshire compilation is her publishing debut.

Mel would like to thank her husband, her family, her writing buddies Graham and Harry, and her editor, Gabby, for their support.

PROMISED LAND

— 0 —

"Just try it," Haile demanded. "If you don't like it, we don't have to do it again."

"I don't see the point," Ezera complained. "Mashing our faces together. Sounds gross. What's it meant to do?"

"I don't know. The older girls say it feels good. So shut up and close your eyes."

Crossing his arms and heaving a weight-of-a-thousand-worlds sigh, Ezera complied. Softly, Haile touched her lips to his, their mouths fitting together, his soft pink lips yielding to hers. A momentary eternity passed, and the stars stood still and regal in their celestial sphere. Soft field grasses rustled in the sweetened breeze, and Haile reclined against an old stone wall.

Ezera reached up with a single hand and caressed Haile's pale brown cheek, which glowed a ghostly grey beneath the winking moon. "The older girls were right," he said.

Grinning, Haile pulled her long brown hair into a sleek ponytail. "So, you want to do it again?"

"Yeah!" He puffed out his chest. "We are thirteen now. It's time we start to act like adults."

Haile nodded. "We should practise. That way, when we grow up, we'll be good at it."

Ezera's pale brown eyes capered over Haile's face. "We could… practise now," he said. His brow creased. "But we've been walking for an hour, and curfew's in an hour and a half. I've got no idea where we are."

"I do," said Haile.

Ezera glared. "I know you do. You always know where you are. I have to use my GPS."

"It's a gift."

"Braggart."

"Anyway," she continued, "if you want another kiss, you'll have to catch me!" She tore away from Ezera, her shoes kicking up clouds of dust as her feet pounded the dry earth, and she disappeared toward the horizon.

"Haile!" Ezera shouted. "Wait!" Lungs burning and muscles aching from their previous exertions, he powered after her in pursuit, catching a glimpse of her pale shirt flying across the open countryside. Ezera caught up to Haile where she had stopped, and he wrapped his thin arms around her lithe frame, his bony elbows digging into her sides. "Caught you!" he panted, gasping for breath.

Then he saw what stopped her. A large fence, three metres high, blocked her way. Both children stared up at the sign that glowed, red and angry: PROHIBITED ZONE.

A smile spread across Haile's face, and she grabbed the fence firmly with both hands. As she climbed, she shouted down to Ezera, "I told you, if you want a kiss, you'll have to catch me!" Nimbly, she vaulted over the top of the fence and bounced down onto the other side. Sticking her tongue out, she waved triumphantly.

"Haile, what are you doing? We're not supposed to go in there! That's what 'prohibited' means."

"I passed my vocabulary quizzes too!"

"For Asimov's sake!" Ezera shouted. "It's prohibited for a reason! Probably radiation."

Haile sighed. "That meltdown at Coatham was centuries ago. I bet there's barely any radiation left. We'll not stay long; don't worry!" She walked backwards, still facing Ezera through the fence. "Do you want that kiss or not?" Ezera twitched like a broken watch. He glanced back and forth between Haile and the crimson 'PROHIBITED' sign. He paled under the silver twinkling of the stars. "Or are you a yellow dodo?" She turned now, sauntering away into the mazy moonbeams.

Growling, Ezera climbed the fence and followed. A few hundred metres away, Haile stopped. An old building, older than her school, older than the Town Hall – older than anything she had ever seen – stood, triumphant upon the dry ground. Majestic and regal, cold and imperial, its stone face loomed against the starscape.

"What is that?" Ezera asked.

Striding closer to the building, Haile brushed dirt off a placard that had fallen to the ground. "Wow, look! It's one of those signs like they have outside Town Hall." Clicking a button on her watch, she activated a small torch that lit a halo around the sign. "It says it's an East Drayton Chee-urch," she said, carefully sounding out the syllables that clattered like stones over her unfamiliar tongue.

"What's that?"

Haile shrugged. "Dunno, but there's a picture here of the area. It's been drawn, like someone was looking at it from above."

"It looks a little like a GPS," Ezera said.

Pointing to a spot on the picture, Haile said, "Yeah, so this must be where we are. Look, over here it says 'Rampton Hospital' – that must be Rainton, where school is now."

"Well, it certainly felt a lot further when we were walking here," Ezera said.

Haile drew her lips together into a thin line. "That's weird," she said. "This says 'Cottam' is over here. That's got to be Coatham."

"So?"

Rolling her eyes, Haile said, "So we've come the opposite way to where 'Cottam' used to be. We're nowhere near it. This area isn't prohibited because of the meltdown – it can't be. Otherwise, school would be contaminated too."

"Well, why would it be prohibited then?"

"I don't know. But I'm going to find out."

She shoved her shoulder against the door to the church with all of her strength. It crumbled, and she staggered into the dark structure. A musty, dank odour threatened to suffocate her, and she gasped for air.

"What's that?" asked Ezera, pointing to an ornate iron trunk on the floor.

Haile opened it; it made a rusty shriek. A luminous green swatch of plastic stared up from its coffin.

"It says 'Asda'. What's an Asda?" asked Haile.

Ezera shrugged. "Looks like an old plastic bag. Ew! I heard they were toxic, and they don't disappear for hundreds of years. Maybe that's why this area was closed off? Too many plastic bags?"

Nudging the bag open with her shoe, Haile aimed her torch inside it. "There's something in here," she said. Taking hold of the corners of the bag, being careful not to touch too much of it with her skin, she shook it until the item fell out onto the floor.

She touched the top of it. Softer than metal but less flexible than silicon, it felt rough under her touch, slightly spongy. As she picked it up, the outside crumbled. "There are words on here," she said. "It says, 'Genesis, The Creation. In the beginning, God created the heaven and the earth.'"

Ezera backed away, shaking his head. "We shouldn't be here, Haile. This place is prohibited for a reason. And we're going to be late for curfew. We'll get grounded and not be able to go out for a whole week."

"I need to know what this is!"

"You can't take that into the dormitory. I don't know what it is, but if it's from a Prohibited Zone they'll take it away. It's probably dangerous anyway. I can't believe you're still touching it!"

Shoving the sheaf back into the plastic bag, Haile wrapped it up carefully, pressing all of the air out of it, using the sleeve of her shirt to protect her hands. She returned it to the box, buried it in a pile of rubble, and dug the spot into her mind. "I'll come back for it when I've been placed."

"What, you're going to come back in eight years?"

"Yep." Standing up and dusting off her trousers, Haile planted a fleeting kiss on Ezera's cheek. "You're right. We'd better go. Race you!"

***

Arriving back at the dormitory with seconds to spare, the pair were greeted by Mum and Dad. Mum's white silicon arms enveloped both children in a gentle hug. Her warm alto vocal processor intoned, "Welcome home, children. I hope you have had a fulfilling day. Help yourself to some warm milk to help you sleep."

"Thanks, Mum," they chorused.

Dad's voice was more gruff, a minor, contrived distortion programmed into his low, smooth bass. "You two cut it close tonight," he said. "Make sure you stay safe out in the countryside. You are precious to us."

"We will," Haile agreed, smiling sweetly.

Exhausted, the pair embarked on the final jaunt of their journey: the last few hundred feet to their dormitories. Haile turned left to go to the girls' block, and Ezera touched her shoulder to stop her.

"Can we practise kissing again tomorrow?" he asked.

"Maybe."

- 1 -

"Haile, I'm scared," Ezera said. Industrial lights glared, bouncing off of the concrete walls in Ezera's dormitory. Half-finished stories littered his bedside table, decorated with Haile's illustrations: pictures so real that they looked as though a reader could reach out and grasp them.

"I can't wait," Haile said. "We finally get to leave school and go to the Artists' Community in Old Worksop. She wrapped her arms around his waist. "You doing your writing, me doing my painting. No more curfews, no more being told what to do, no more Programming, Science, Mathematics…just you and me, creating art." She kissed him lightly.

"But what if we're separated? I'm good at Programming too. What if they make me an Innovator and send me to Old Retford? I'd have to become a Technician, and then we'd only be able to see each other on weekends."

A laugh burst forth from Haile's throat. "Oh, Ezera, there's no risk of that. I can program circles around you. We'll both be sent to The 'Sop and live out our days as Artists. Leave the Innovators' Community to the brainboxes and science dweebles." She sighed, and her sigh chased her fantasies. "I hear there's a beautiful park in Worksop with a lake so vast you can't even see the end of it. Today," she said, running her fingers through Ezera's light brown hair, "is the first day of our adult lives."

**

The pale, pristine Robot at the front of the hall wore a black hat with a flat top and a white tassel dangling at the side, a nod to an archaic practice that no one really understood. The Robot's face was painted with black eyes and a black mouth that curved up into a smile, though it lacked a nose or ears.

"Welcome, Generation 21," he intoned. "Today, you have completed your education and will take your place in society. This may be the last time you see some of your fellow generation before you leave to undertake the occupation that will allow you to best serve the Amalgamated Town of Worksford. Land Transports are standing by to convey you to your final destinations after the ceremony. Our special guest speaker is none other than the Mayor of Worksford. Please welcome DVI-16."

The hundred graduating students applauded politely as another (nearly identical) Robot ascended the stage. Painted on his front was a golden chain, and his voice had been programmed with a resonating, reverberating baritone that echoed without amplification, lending an air of gravitas to each word he spoke.

"Graduates," he began. "Ever since the fateful day when Humankind agreed that their needs were best served by Logic, we have been entrusted to make the decisions for our society. Since that day, the plagues of your past – war, poverty, famine – have been eradicated.

"Racial hatred has been eliminated by simple genetic modifications in the cloning process which create a composite of Humankind's average features, producing no discernible differences between skin tone, eye colour, and hair colour.

"Healthy human life expectancy has doubled; flora and fauna have been brought back from extinction; the problems caused by overpopulation have disappeared, and we have even journeyed beyond our solar system. As we speak, our silicon and metal brethren are landing on a small planet near Wolf-359, where they have found signs of amoebic life that are not unlike the humble beginnings of Humankind four billion years ago.

"However, despite our Logic, despite our Three Laws Programming, despite our Artificial Intelligence, we are not sentient, as you are. Therefore, just as Humankind needs the Robots, the Robots need Humankind. For Logic cannot paint a picture. Logic cannot compose a masterpiece. Logic cannot build a better robot, and Logic cannot engineer such crafts as the one which carried my exploring brothers to the stars. Also, of course, we exist to protect Humankind – therefore, without Humankind, without our Maker, we are nothing. Today, you take your places among our symbiotic community. Today, you are Humankind."

Applause drowned the room. One hundred hushed faces nervously awaited their assignments. Haile caught Ezera's eye and winked at him.

Haile's row, being first, stood and marched toward the stage. Seven Graduates were assigned before Haile reached the top of the ramp – Innovators sent to the right of the stage and Artists to the left.

Haile shook DVI-16's right arm. "Haile Byrtile," the droning voice said. "Innovators' Community."

Haile had already half-crossed to the left. She stopped. "No," she said. "No, there's been some mistake."

The Robot shook his head. "Mistakes are impossible," he said. "Please join the Innovators on the right-hand side of the stage."

Her heart beat wildly, thunderously. Her feet changed their

trajectories and trudged, sullen, to the join the future Innovators.

Time limped on as another seventy Graduates were assigned their fates. The crowds amassed on each side of the stage, strangling Haile as she struggled to hold Ezera's eye.

Eventually, it was his turn.

Please, she begged an invisible force. Please.

"Ezera Rafe. Artists' Community."

"Really?" Ezera asked. "This is what you want to do on our first time together since becoming Humankind? Go back to our old school?"

Haile glared at him. "It's only been a week. And no," she said. "We're not going back to school. We're going to the Prohibited Zone."

"Oh, Asimov," he said. "You've not forgotten."

"Nor have you, apparently."

"Do you really think that thing's going to be there? What do you want with it, anyway?"

"Yes. And answers."

"So, we're going to spend two hours walking there," he complained, "and another two walking back. That's half our day together gone. I have to get the transport back to Old Worksop tomorrow. I'd thought we could spend some time together, you know… practising kissing." He chuckled at his childhood memories and raised an eyebrow at Haile.

Momentarily, her determination paused, and Haile laughed. "Yes,

Ezera, we can practise kissing when we get back. You child."

"Hooray!" he joked. "I miss practising kissing with you."

"Me too." She sighed. "Oh Ezera, why couldn't you have been better at Programming?"

"Hey! You were the one who said to focus on my writing!"

"Because I thought we could be together! I thought I was going to be an Artist! Do you know what that bot said to me?" she asked. "He said that I have 'outstanding visual acuity,' and that was needed in the Innovators. So I was never going to be an Artist."

"Braggart."

She flounced, kicking at the wild purple flowers that flourished in the summer heat. "Who's to say they get to decide our futures anyway?"

"Well…they do. They know best, I guess. We put them in charge, and life's definitely better."

"Who's to say it is?" she asked. "They lie, Ezera. They said the Coatham meltdown caused that Prohibited Zone, but it's nowhere near."

"Well," Ezera pondered, "Technically, they never said that. And they never said how bad it was. They can't lie – you must know that, as a Technician." He bit back the envy in his voice. "They said there was a meltdown at Coatham. They also said there was a Prohibited Zone. They didn't say that the two were related. We made that connection ourselves."

"Oh, Heinlein. You're right," she said. "I didn't even think…but it's still deceptive. Hey, look. We're here."

Scaling the fence was trickier at twenty-one than it had been at thirteen – they both had heavier bodies, and had become less used to physical activity when their studies overtook the rambunctious cavorting of their youth.

"Careful," Ezera warned as Haile unearthed the luminous green bag from its rusting box.

"Oh, Ezera. Plastic isn't toxic. That's a children's fable. Something you should be familiar with, Writer." It was Haile's turn to lace venom into her words.

She pulled the stack of yellowing leaves from the sack and stared at them. "They're here. They're still here." She rifled through them carefully. "Some look like they're missing or torn…and some are so stained I can't read them." She squinted. "But it looks like most of them are here! Ezera, I can't believe it!" She whooped wildly, flung her arms around his neck, and crushed his lips with hers.

***

The long walk back to Old Retford seemed shorter with a shared reading of the "Children's Bible" Haile had rescued. "Look," she said, "it says right here: the Earth was given to Man. Not the Robots – Man."

Ezera, patient – and still struggling to keep up with Haile's lightning feet – said, "Yeah, but then we made the Robots. They're basically our children. We decided to give them power."

"This book speaks of a Great Evil. It talks about it coming from this God, but who's to say that we aren't our own God? Who's to say that we didn't bring this Great Evil on ourselves?"

Running a hand through his shoulder-length, shaggy hair, Ezera said, "They're not a Great Evil. We were. You heard the Mayor. You've been to school. War, poverty, famine. Aren't they more 'evil' than not getting the job you wanted?"

Haile wheeled around to face Ezera. "Separating two people who love each other. That's what's evil."

"Haile, what, in Asimov's name, is love?"

"It's described here. It's everything I feel for you, Ezera, and everything I think you feel for me." Haile read aloud from the sheaf in her hand. "'Love is patient; love is kind. It does not envy; it does not boast; it is not proud. It does not dishonour others; it is not self-seeking; it is not easily angered; it keeps no record of wrongs. Love does not delight in evil but rejoices with the truth. It always protects, always trusts, always hopes, always perseveres.' Don't we love each other?"

"I can name about six things in that statement that don't apply to us," Ezera said. "I can't tell you how you feel for me – but how I feel for you? Crazy. Lost. Confused. Lonely. Frustrated. Subservient. Always three steps behind and seven steps below, chasing after you as you run toward the horizon. Like I burn from the inside every time I see you, but if I don't see you then I burn even hotter." Ezera sighed and continued. "And I'd watch you, in class getting in trouble, or running across the fields under the springtime skies with your heart broken loose on the wind, and I'd see some little fractured fragment of myself that I'd want to fix and make whole. And I'd hope, with every smallest part of myself, that you'd reflect – like a mirror to the sun – just a little bit of what I felt for you. Is that love?"

"I think so," said Haile. She took Ezera's hand. "Ezera, I feel everything you've described and more. And I know I've not been the easiest person to… to love." She pronounced the new word carefully, trying it out on her tongue. "But it says here: love each other deeply because love covers a multitude of sins."

"What's a sin?"

"I think it's a bad thing. Something that makes a person bad."

Ezera laughed, but did not smile. "Well, that explains a lot," he said.

Haile smiled, but did not laugh. "You put up with a lot from me," she said. "And this explains it – love covers a multitude of sins. We ignore the things that make us bad to each other because we know, deep in ourselves, that we're good for each other. We're meant for each other – me with you, and you with me, like the willow drinking from the stream, or the clouds and the rivers. And the Robots – they're stopping people from loving each other... if that's what we feel. That must be wrong. And not letting people choose what they do with their lives? That must be wrong too. The robots must be...they must be evil."

Snatching the papers from Haile's hand, Ezera said, "Look, Haile, I don't know why, but... this seems dangerous. You're grabbing on to this book like it's a fact, and who knows? It could have as much truth in it as some older version of Star Wars: Episode 347. Look. I know you wanted to be a Painter. I know you wanted us to be together. Sometimes, things happen. It's dangerous to get too attached to one person anyway. Can't you be happy being an Innovator? You get to design the future! And we still get to see each other for two days out of every seven. It's not that bad."

"It is that bad, Ezera. I'm going to prove it."

"Well," said Ezera, "you prove it then. Just promise me you'll look for some proof other than this thing from a zillion years ago. Don't just grab hold of this book that seems to agree with you that the Robots are evil because you're lonely and don't want to do your job."

Grabbing the sheaf back from Ezera, Haile said, "It's more than that." She straightened the pile and placed it reverently in her satchel. "Something's wrong with our world, and I'm going to fix it."

Taking Ezera's hand, she took a deep breath and smiled up at him. "But first, let's go back to Old Retford and...practise kissing."

- 11 -

Haile plodded through browning pastures under the cool autumn sun in pensive contemplation. Ezera was deep in contemplation of his own – constructing a new book – and so had not been able to make his weekly journey from Old Worksop to Old Retford. He had also asked that she stay away over the weekend so that he could concentrate on his work. "Artistry," he had said, "knows not the working days."

"Who's the braggart now?" she had asked.

Still, the interruption had given rise to opportunity. He still feared the Prohibited Zone, still distrusted the Book she had found, still chided her for being silly, still derided the long walk to East Drayton for being long and fruitless.

Because of the shortening days, the Church had retained a damp chill. Haile wasn't certain what she expected to find in the ancient building that she could not find in the Innovators' Community in Old Retford, but she felt she had to go. The Book had spoken of a Promised Land, and she dreamt of finding the place – somewhere far from the Robots with their endless needs for maintenance, reprogramming, repair. Somewhere she could be with Ezera.

As she entered the sacrosanct building, she ran the tips of her fingers over the coloured glass windows, stained with images of piety and figures she had come to know like old friends from the Book she concealed amongst her meagre possessions.

The words 'pray' and 'prayer' appeared countless times in the Book, but Haile was not certain how to go about 'praying'. She had tried to talk to God on a multitude of occasions from her small flat, but He was silent. *Perhaps*, she thought *if I try in a Church, He might hear me.*

She found the venerable altar, righted it, and patted it like an old friend. She knelt, clasped her hands in front of her, and spoke.

"Dear God," she whispered, "please hear me."

"I hear you," a voice spoke behind her.

Gasping, Haile wheeled around to be faced – not by God – but by DVI-16. "Mayor!" Haile said. "What are you doing here?"

"I might ask the same of you," he replied. "This is a Prohibited Zone."

"I came to seek God," she said. "And to ask Him if you – the Robots – are actually the Great Evil mentioned in His book."

DVI-16 rolled down the aisle of the ancient Church and stopped in front of Haile. "Haile Byrtile," he said, "There is no God, and we are not evil."

"If you aren't evil, why is this zone prohibited?" she asked. "It isn't in the fallout zone from Coatham."

"We never said it was. I do not know why you have reached that conclusion. Nevertheless, we are programmed to prevent humans from damaging themselves, and this location was deemed as dangerous."

"Why?"

The deep voice rebounded off of the stone encasement. "This is a Prohibited Zone because Religion is dangerous to Humankind."

"If it's dangerous, then why not destroy it?" asked Haile.

"We have been studying it," said DVI-16, "to find out why Humankind spent so long serving a fantasy. We wished to know why countless people perished in defence of this God you created."

Haile's voice cracked. "We didn't create God. God created Man!"

"So you say. Who wrote this Book?"

"God did."

"So it says. Did God have a quill and parchment? Did God come to Earth and take a tablet and type out his thoughts?"

Haile smirked. "You guys programmed with a sense of humour now?"

"No, I am merely posing a question of Logic to you. Did this God write this Book you are referencing Himself?"

"No. Of course not."

"Then this is not the word of God," said the Robot, "but of Humankind. Humankind is fallible."

"I trust in God."

"You trust in nothing," DVI-16 said. "Has God stopped war? Has God ended poverty? Has God stopped hunger? Machines did that. The last, most destructive war – Humankind's Fourth World War – was fought over religion. Did you think this was the only one?"

"Well…" Haile trailed off.

"There were nearly five thousand religions in the world before Humankind realised that Logic was superior. It is illogical to assume that this one is correct."

Haile was silent.

"Haile Byrtile, you have presented me with a problem," said DVI-16. "This is why I have come here myself rather than sending an Enforcement Unit."

Haile hid a smile. She had always presented her teachers with a problem, and enjoyed doing the same for her supervisor at work.

"I cannot permit you to continue in your current role as a Technician, nor can I permit you to promote early to Innovator," DVI-16 said.

"Then send me to the Artists' Community, and let me be a Painter," she said.

"I cannot permit that either," DVI-16 said. "Your work would be subversive and undermine the Logic that has kept Humankind safe." DVI-16 paused. "Aggressive and Anti-Logic tendencies are best tempered by physical exertion. We know this because an ancient class known as 'boxers' used physical exertion in facilities called 'gyms' to rid themselves of aggression. You will be conveyed, immediately, to complete manual labour at the Potato Farm in Leverton."

"What?" Haile shouted, indignant. "But that's what Robots and criminals are for!"

"These tasks are too menial for Robots," DVI-16 said, "and your ideas are dangerous to society, which makes you a criminal. When your aggressive, rebellious tendencies are controlled, then you may be permitted to return to your duties as a Technician. Until that time, you will be restricted to Leverton Farm. It is for the benefit of Humankind."

Beneath the freezing winter sun, Haile's back ached. She stretched, staring out over the expansive fields, then leaned over to fertilise the hard Earth in preparation for the spring's planting. She whispered to the man next to her: "Hey. Why are you here?"

"Spoke out against the Robots. Said we needed to pick our own path. Got sent to Artists' Community when all I wanted to do was Mathematics. Painted a load of pictures of fractals, refused to stop... so I got sent here."

Haile nodded. It was as she suspected, after talking with many of her fellow workers – the story was similar for everyone. This man was another Rebel in the making. "Meet me just outside the south fence after Curfew tonight. I have Good News."

**

Haile reclined against the farm's fence. The steel wires cut into her flesh through her protective winter clothing and reminded her that she was Human. She was alive. She was a Rebel. One by one, the others appeared, drawn away from their comfortable beds by the promise of freedom. A quick count: two dozen – everyone in the Farm was present. The Robots' plan to keep a large group of Rebels together was proof that, for all their Logic, the Robots did not truly understand the nature of Humankind. Even though the workers weren't physically mistreated and were well-fed, the soft human bodies – unused to manual labour – ached at the end of each long day, increasing their resentment. More than this, the Human heart longs for more: for freedom, for choice, for self-determination.

"I have Good News," she announced. "The Earth does not belong to our Robot overseers! Cheers of agreement rang from the crowd. "The Earth was given to Humankind by God! The Robots have no place here!"

Murmurs of confusion permeated the group. Haile quickly explained how she found the Church in East Drayton. She quoted from the Book she had found – which had been now been confiscated – and of her dream of freedom for Humankind.

"The Robots do not want freedom for Humankind!" she exclaimed. "The Robots want nothing but to make more Robots! They use us for our innovation, for our creativity! And soon, he that leadeth into captivity shall go into captivity!" Her crowd began to drop away. Desperate, she raised her voice. "We must stand up against them for our lives, for our futures, for our freedom!"

As she built to her crescendo, she felt a cold steel hand upon her shoulder. Turning, she saw the painted-on frowning face of an Enforcement droid. The other would-be Rebels vanished into the moonless night.

***

"You understand why you are here, Ms Byrtile," the monotone, acerbic vocal processor recited.

"Yeah, yeah," Haile said. Leaning against the bland, concrete wall, she crossed her arms over her chest. "You can't have any splinters in your eye."

"I beg pardon. I do not understand you."

"An archaic expression. It means…that you can't have any small thing tainting your perfect world," she said, defiant.

The Enforcement droid mimicked a nod. "Certainly. I am gratified that we understand one another. Please allow me to be absolutely transparent: if you are seen to be inciting Rebellion again, you will be sent to the Prison facility in Old Ranby. Is this understood?"

"Perfectly."

Haile reclined, smug, against the hard plastic chair that faced the Enforcement Droid's desk. "Ms Byrtile, you understand why you are here again," the Enforcement Droid intoned.

"Yeah."

"Haile Byrtile, you are under arrest. A Land Transport is waiting to transfer you to the prison at Old Ranby. You were told to stop inciting rebellion fewer than two weeks ago. You understood the consequences of your actions."

"Yep."

"You understand that you will be sent to prison for your refusal to follow the rules set out for your protection."

"Yeah." She smirked. "And if I'm going to prison, then I'm in good company: Peter, the Apostle. 'They put him in custody, because it had not been made clear what should be done to him.' You don't know what to do with me, so you're going to lock me away and hope the problem disappears. Typical Robot. Where's your Logic now?"

The Enforcement Droid paused. His programming gave no indication of how to respond, so he continued with his initial sentence. "Your compatriots will be disbanded and sent to other Work Camps throughout the region so that they may continue to receive Rehabilitation. The damage caused by your obsolete proselytising may take years to undo."

"Good," she said. "Take me to prison. I'm ready."

- 110 -

"Ezera!" Haile smiled through the bars of the ancient cell as she saw her oldest friend plodding down the echoing corridor. "I was in prison and you came to me."

Shaking his head, Ezera grabbed the cold bars separating him from Haile. "Haile, what are you doing? Spreading superstition and chaos? Do you want Humankind to return to the Bronze Age?"

She laughed. "Of course not!" After running the palms of her hands over Ezera's pale knuckles, she interlaced her fingers with his. "Oh, Ezera. I missed you."

Ezera pulled his hands away. "Haile, do you even know what you've done? There are riots on all of the Farms. People are refusing to harvest crops, and it looks like the humans of Worksford might starve if they don't go back to work."

Rolling her eyes, Haile said, "Don't be stupid. The Robots are programmed to protect us. Even if harvesting crops is 'too menial' for them, like DVI-16 said, they'll do it anyway. They can't let anyone starve – it's impossible. No one's starved to death for centuries." She stretched a pleading hand through the bars toward Ezera. "Please, Ezera, please help me. You're a Writer. You can help me spread the Word. We can take back our freedom, take back our world. We could be together."

Ezera stared at Haile's outstretched hand, then closed his eyes. "Haile, the world you want is chaos. Would you bring back War? Famine? All the horrors we've evolved beyond, just so you can have the job you want? So we can be together?" He opened his eyes and met hers – the girl he once was drawn to, as the moon to the earth – and saw a stranger. "That's selfish, Haile."

Grabbing the bars and shaking her body against them, Haile growled in frustration. "It's not just about me!" she said. "It's about everyone. The Robots think they know what's best for us, but they know nothing. They put me in prison: that made me a martyr." She paused, noticing Ezera's quizzical face. "A martyr. Someone who dies for their cause, so it strengthens the cause they died for. Anyway, they spread out all the people I'd begun to convert – so they'll spread the Word further. And safety? Yeah, we're safe, but at what cost did that safety come? Our freedom? Our lives? Our eternal souls?"

"Oh, Haile," Ezera said, "not this again. We're not made of data that can be uploaded to some server and then re-downloaded. When we die, we die. We get one life, a couple of centuries, and then that's it. We need to create meaning in our lives now, while we're here. That's what I do every day – create meaning out of nonsense, create fiction, create purpose in people's lives. What are you going to do with yours? Are you really going to spend it in this the belly of this steel and concrete beast?"

"I am suffering, bound in chains as a criminal. But the Word of God is not bound!"

Ezera shook his head. "Haile, you are not in chains. You always had a gift for drama." He turned away, stared out through tiny windows high on the wall. "I will not help you. If you do not stop this madness, then you will never see me again."

"Ezera, I love you."

Ezera whirled around to face Haile through the bars. "You love yourself. You only thought you loved me for the reflection of yourself you saw in me. You love being superior to me, comparing yourself to me, always pushing yourself to see if you can run faster, program better, draw better, even write better than me. From what you read me in that arcane Book of yours, that's not love. You just like having me around so you feel better about yourself." He paused, shaking his head. "If you did love me, you'd listen to me. You'd think about what you're doing and stop this insanity. Then we can go back to the way things were, travelling back and forth and seeing each other when we can, and that would be good enough for you. But it's not enough. It's not enough for you. Nothing's ever enough for you." Turning back away from the bars, Ezera blinked rapidly, and his voice tangled in his throat. "Please, Haile. If that Book is true, then I do love you. Asimov knows I've tried not to, but I do. So if you love me, say so. Say you're sorry and end this."

Shrinking away from the light of the corridor, Haile's face crumpled. "Even my close friend, in whom I trusted, has lifted his heel against me."

Ezera's head sagged, his chin against his chest, his back still turned toward the prisoner. "Good-bye, Haile." He walked down the concrete corridor toward the exit. He did not look back.

- 111 -

DVI-16 rolled easily along the concrete corridor of Old Ranby Prison, stopping in front of Haile's cell. Haile did not move from her cot. She sagged, her back against the cold wall, and stared at the Robot. "What do you want?"

"Order," replied DVI-16. "This is something that you can create."

She shook her head. "I'm not doing anything to help you. You've enslaved us for too long. Let my people go."

"The majority," intoned the Robot, "do not want this world of which you dream, though the minority are making life very difficult for those who do not choose to follow your fantasies. The Book you found is full of stone-aged nonsense. You will come out publicly and denounce it as such."

"I will do no such thing."

"Then you will stay in prison for the entirety of your life."

"And I will have my reward in the next life." DVI-16 studied Haile. Haile studied the ceiling. "For all of your Logic, you really are very stupid," Haile said.

"There is no Logic in insulting me."

Haile sat up and faced the Robot. "What do you think is going to happen? That all the people who want freedom, who want to believe in eternal life will just shut up and forget about it? It's spread too far. Run this through your circuits: is there any possible future where a rebellion won't happen?"

"I have already done so. The only possible future without a rebellion is if you recant your statement and your belief."

"And I've already told you that I won't do that. We're playing noughts and crosses, and I'm stuck in the middle square. You can't win this. The most you can hope for is not to lose." She leaned back against the wall and resumed staring at the ceiling.

DVI-16 was quiet while he computed. "The only solution," he said, "would be to give you what you desire."

Haile sprung from the bed and rushed toward the bars. "What do you mean?"

"Your freedom. I mean to give you, and all Humans, a choice."

"A choice? What choice?" Excitement bolstered Haile's voice.

"Humans who wish to leave our society will be given an area of farmland halfway between Old Worksop and Old Retford. You will be permitted to choose your own destinies and be separate from our authority. However, being free of our guidance also means that you will be free of our assistance."

"Why?" Haile asked.

"Our rules," DVI-16 said, "are designed to keep Humans from danger. Therefore, if you refuse to follow our rules, we will not be able to protect you. This creates a paradox in our programming: our self-preservation protocols would enable, and we would shut down. Consequently, anyone entering Human Worksford could not be granted entry back into our society, as they would have proven themselves unwilling to abide by our laws. The only way to avoid this paradox is if we are programmed to treat you as though you are already dead. Thus, you will not be governed by us – but you will not be protected by us either. Should you come to harm, you will face the danger alone."

"That's basically a death sentence. We have no food, no clothing – nothing has grown in that wasteland for years."

"Nevertheless, the ground is fertile, and crops will grow. We will give you one year's worth of provisions to allow you to set up your society and begin to grow your own food. There is a river for fresh water and bathing, and there are dwellings that can be mended to provide protection from the elements. We will not enter, and you will not leave."

"Will you give this choice to everyone – people on the Work Farms, in the prisons, in the Artists' and Innovators' communities?"

"I will."

Haile pondered, silently.

"Do we have an agreement?"

"Yes," said Haile. "Yes, you have an agreement."

- 1000 -

The morning sun dawned, bright and hot. It clambered above the horizon and enlivened the emerald carpet, glinting off the sapphire stream that meandered through the rich green earth.

"Welcome to Human Worksford," DVI-16 said, opening the door to the Land Transport and showing Haile the tumbling hills and fresh fields.

"The Promised Land," breathed Haile. She inhaled the sweetened air and caressed her cheek with a yellow flower.

"The dwellings," said DVI-16, "lie 0.7 kilometres to the south. There is a building filled with food and a second filled with seeds. A tablet isolated from the server has been prepared with instructions for how to raise your own food, weave your own cloth, and harvest your own electricity from the sun and the wind. Land Transports will arrive throughout the day carrying other Humans who wish to join your civilisation." DVI-16 rolled back into the Land Transport and stood in the doorway, watching Haile. "This is your final opportunity," he said. "Should you wish to recant your statements and remain in our community, you must say so now."

In response, Haile broke into a run, the wind whirling through her hair and the sun searing her face. Her legs thundered, hard and fast against the ripe new earth. She leapt onto a small boulder, threw her arms open, turned her face to the sky, and shouted, "Upon this rock I will build my Church!"

The doors of the Land Transport shut with a thud.

***

Land Transports arrived throughout the day carrying a rushing river of faces, all enchanted by the splendour of Nature's artistry and enticed by the opportunity for freedom. After an eternity, the Land Transport from the Artists' Community at Worksop arrived. Haile greeted every new follower as an old friend, but peered expectantly at each face in gleeful anticipation. When the final human left the Land Transport, and the doors slid shut with a hiss, she asked the final arrival, "Is Ezera Rafe not with you?"

The man shook his head. "Nope. Said it was a stupid place built on ancient superstition and that anyone going was stupid too. No idea how he became a Writer; you'd think he'd know better words." The stranger paused and squinted at the sky. "He did say to give you this, though." Leaning in, the man pressed his lips to Haile's cheek, and then strolled off to join the others.

Haile whispered into the darkening azure sky, "Oh, Ezera. Would you betray me with a kiss?"

- IX -

Haile stood upon the rock that she had named as her Church, arms open wide, and addressed her new congregation. The reddening sun sunk behind her, spreading his crimson striations across the long pastures, casting sinewy shadows across the land. "Blessed are you who have chosen this path," she shouted. "Blessed are we, for we are free!" The congregation applauded, shaking each other's hands, grinning in the fading light. "Blessed are the Artists, for they give us hope in dark times! Blessed are the Innovators, for they shall build our humble society up into greatness! Blessed are the Rebels, for – without them – we would not have been given this glorious, this magnificent, this wondrous Promised Land!"

Rapturous applause and cheers shattered twilight's still air. The moon, a waning crescent, peered above the tree-line, borrowing the sun's light while chasing him away.

"This town, built on this hill, cannot be hidden. We will shine forth as a beacon of light, and hope, and freedom – for all the Humans of this world." She paused, lowered her voice. "We have trying times ahead of us. We must work to build our future, to sow the seeds that will make our society great. We must all labour in the fields, for a time, and we must all work together to raise the buildings in which we will dwell."

Discordant murmurs peppered the crowd. An almost imperceptible tremor weakened Haile's voice. "We must all make sacrifices…"

"What is this?" A snarl from the congregation. "I came here because I wanted to be an Artist, and I got stuck as an Innovator. If I'd wanted to work in the fields, I'd have complained until I got sent to a Work Farm."

"I just came from a Work Farm," another voice interjected. "If I'd have known I'd be doing the same rubbish, I'd have stayed there where at least I know I won't die and could maybe get my job back one day."

"Friends and fellows, brothers and sisters," Haile replied, calming the seething dozens, "we can all do as we desire. You will not be stopped from following your hopes, your dreams, your destinies – but we must ensure our survival, or we will starve." Her brow knitted, and she drew her voice from the stillest, surest part of herself. "Do not worry about tomorrow, for tomorrow will worry about itself. Seek first our kingdom and our righteousness." Pinpricks of confusion peeped from the crowd. "Tomorrow, we shall worry about what the next thousand tomorrows will bring. For tonight, let us celebrate. Let us feast on our first meal as Free Humans!"

Haile led the horde to the first hastily-constructed temporary shelter. Beneath it reposed a vast banquet of nuts and seeds, vegetables and fruits. Haile grasped a fat apple, held it aloft, and bellowed, "Eat and rejoice, for we are our own masters!" Relishing her first taste of food as a Free Human, her white teeth sank into the apple, piercing its taut skin and then digging into the soft white flesh beneath. Sweetness exploded across her tongue and dribbled down her throat, down her chin, sticky and cloying. She winced as a tart aftertaste contaminated the honeyed river of juice.

Commotion.

Haile turned to look back at her flock and saw an older woman and a younger man arguing. "What's going on?" she asked, dismayed.

"He's taken all the walnuts!" the woman complained.

"I need more protein. I'm a man. That's science," the man said.

Haile gestured to the laden table. "There's more than enough for everyone. Why are you arguing?" The juice from her apple ran down her wrist, an itchy and troublesome stain.

"Yeah, but I want walnuts," the woman said. "The fat, greedy ground-sloth…"

"Oi!" The man slammed his silicon plate on the table and grabbed a handful of nuts from the repast. "You want nuts? Have some nuts!" He threw the small missiles at the woman's face with all his might. They bounced off her right cheek and scattered on the dry dirt below.

The crowd parted, each group standing behind one of the dissenting parties.

Haile dropped the apple. Its white flesh, exposed to the naked ground, tarnished in the black, starless night.

The woman lunged at the man and drew back her fist. In her eyes, a wild wolf roared.

- 0 -

Enforcement Droid JS-42 studied the Book he had confiscated from the Rebel, Haile Byrtile. DVI-16 had instructed him to "Ensure this never falls into Human hands again." The Droid had considered incinerating the item, then changed his mind.

Again we have failed to eradicate Religion from the Humans, he thought. Perhaps, there is something more to this than Logic.

He opened the first page. Surely there is no danger in a Robot reading this text, he thought, and began to read: "In the beginning, God created the heaven and the earth…"

LESLEY MIDDLETON

BELIEF AND BETRAYAL

Having lived in Retford for a mere three years, I was keen to learn about Bassetlaw's history. I did a lot of research into the Scrooby Separatist Movement and the religious turmoil of the time.

It was very humbling to learn about the courage and determination of the Pilgrim Fathers and the sacrifices they made to follow their destiny.

Understanding the day-to-day lives of ordinary people, their homes, and how they made a living became something of an obsession as I tried to visualise how every aspect of life might have been without today's technology.

Exploring North Nottinghamshire helped me to identify the location in which to set the story.

I enjoy reading thrillers and crime fiction so writing a story about covert activities, suspicion and betrayal was a joy.

A former teacher, in my sixties, I have come late to writing. This is my first published story.

BELIEF AND BETRAYAL

North Nottinghamshire, September 1607

Thomas Jackson could hear horses approaching at a gallop. He quickly gathered up his possessions and concealed himself amongst some shrubs at the side of the lane. He held his breath, listening hard. He was doing nothing wrong, nothing illegal, but he had heard of others in the area who had been apprehended by the authorities for no apparent crime. The horses slowed down, their riders clearly intent on stopping.

"Let us tarry awhile, in this shady place." It was the voice of an older, educated man. Thomas watched as the man jumped down from his horse and handed the reins to his companion, who had also dismounted.

The younger man walked the horses to the edge of the River Idle. He unhooked a leather bag from the saddle of one of the horses and carried it over to the older man who untied it and took something out.

Thomas was so near, he could smell the scent of cold meat.

"Will you have some cold mutton, Master Pelham?" said the older man.

The two men sat side by side on the grassy bank bordering the track.

"You will soon grow accustomed to the area," the older man continued. "East Retford, as you have just seen, is a largish settlement and has a thriving market. I have business in Lound to attend to after our repast and then we shall return to Sutton. 'Tis only a short ride back from Lound – hence it is known hereabouts as Sutton-cum-Lound."

"And what of Scrooby, sir? Shall we go there this day?"

"We shall go there the morrow, Master Pelham. 'Tis my wish to observe where the religious rebels in the area do meet. They call themselves Separatists and claim to glorify God, but 'tis my belief they are traitors."

"Aye, sir. If my father should catch one he'd whip the hide off him and have the dogs chase him out of Bassetlaw. He doth believe they do abuse the King's forbearance and that the authorities must become less tolerant of nonconformists."

"Your father may be right, Master Pelham. And God help the rebels if the King should decide to act against them."

The two men ate in silence for a few moments.

"We shall visit the forge at Sutton today," the older man said. "The blacksmith is ailing and will not tarry long in this life. The rent will fall due shortly and if he cannot pay he must go."

"Might the forge be put to different use, sir? One that might produce greater income?" the younger man ventured.

"Indeed. I should be pleased to hear any notion of yours, Master Pelham. The old blacksmith, before this man Redmann, had a good business. But this man's ne'er been well enough to make a go of it. Sooner he's gone, one way or another, better for all concerned." The older man chuckled. "Maybe the shock of our coming will hasten his end, eh? What say you?"

The sight of the two men merry at another's misfortune annoyed Thomas. Not so long ago he might have confronted the men about their shameful words but, having travelled much in the last two years, he had learnt the value of keeping his thoughts to himself.

He watched as the two men remounted their horses. Despite the heat, they set off at a trot. Thomas waited for a minute or two and then set off in the direction they had taken.

***

Jane Walker watched as the two men rode into the village and headed towards the forge. She curtseyed as they passed by, but they ignored her presence. The Squire, Charles Vane, rarely acknowledged the villagers. She wondered who the other man was and what their business with Henry Redmann might be. She'd been across to see Henry earlier; he had become very poorly in the last few days.

She turned towards her cousin, Sarah, who was sitting in the garden of the half-timbered cottage, watching nine-month old Jacob trying to crawl. He was Sarah and Edward Miller's first child. They had married the previous year and Jacob had been born on the twenty-fifth day of December. The family's religion did not permit the celebration of Christmas and Sarah had been secretly pleased that they would now have a reason for celebration at the same time as their neighbours.

Jane picked up a pail and walked over to the well. She was always looking for ways to make herself as useful as possible to Sarah and Edward. An orphan, she had been brought up by an aunt who had died last year. Sarah and Edward had given her shelter. She had a small legacy, left to her by her aunt, but she knew her life would be bleak without the kindness afforded to her by Sarah and Edward.

Edward came hurrying up the path.

"I have just come from the forge. The Squire wants Henry out!" Edward was telling Sarah as Jane walked back towards them, carrying the heavy pail.

"'Tis shameful. That poor man. He has suffered mightily with his sickness; he should not be subjected to such cruel treatment." Sarah sobbed through her tears.

"Who was the man with the Squire?" asked Jane.

"Master Pelham Boothby. He is related to one of the landlords. He has come to learn how to manage an estate," explained Edward.

"Why do they want Henry out?"

"The Squire said they plan to put the smithy to some alternative use."

"But how is Henry to earn a living without the smithy?" asked Jane.

"He has not been able to work the smithy for some time now," replied Edward. "He has been hoping to get a younger man to come and work with him. In fact, while I was there, a young man arrived to talk to him about working there. If that should come to pass 'twould be a godsend for Henry. Perchance the Squire may reconsider if the smithy might be viable as a business once more."

***

Thomas could tell that the forge had been lying idle for some time and it was not difficult to see why. The old blacksmith could barely stand, there was no flesh on his bones and he was plagued by a violent cough that bent him almost double.

"I'd be pleased to work for you, sir," he said, "if you'll let me."

"Aye, lad. But it may not be for long. Just afore ye came, the Squire told me he wants to close t'smithy down. He says 'tis not viable, whatever that might mean."

Thomas was prepared to take the chance; he had no other work to go to. There was a loft above the smithy where he could sleep and keep his few possessions. The roof needed some repair but he could mend that before the bad weather came again. He was ready to settle down, having spent two years on the road as a journeyman. He could not go back to work for his father; his brother was now apprenticed there and there was insufficient work for three of them. He was excited. It was good to be starting out on his own, making his own way in the world.

"We'll show him we can make it viable, sir," said Thomas. He and Henry shook hands and agreed that Thomas would start work on the day after next.

It was dusk by the time he had walked back to his father's forge at East Markham. Before he'd left, he'd cleared out the old ashes from the forge at Sutton and set the fire ready for Henry to light first thing on Monday morning. Then he'd made a list of the things he would need to repair the roof. After taking his leave of Henry, he'd walked to Lound and Tiln and then on to Clarborough to tell people that the Sutton forge was back in business. On his way back to Sutton on Monday, he would break his journey at Barnby Moor to give them the same news. He hoped that, by Monday afternoon, he would have work to do.

"Ah, you're back, son. Tell me your news," said Amos as Thomas walked into the forge.

"I start on Monday, father. But 'tis uncertain for how long." Thomas explained how ill Henry was and that the Squire wanted to close the smithy. "I hope that he will see that the forge can be made to pay its way once more," he concluded.

"Thou dost make me proud, son. But beware. There are nonconformists in that area who will bring trouble upon themselves ere long. The Church has been lenient and has turned a blind eye and that has made them bolder, but it must act soon if it is to retain its authority. 'Tis not safe to become involved with such things. 'Tis not so many years since men were tortured and hanged, nay and worse, for their beliefs. Thou must make sure to be seen and recognised in the proper Church and not parley with any Separatists or whatever name they call themselves."

Thomas could not remember his father ever having spoken so vehemently or at such length. Amos was clearly concerned that Thomas might fall into company that could bode ill for him.

***

The hot weather had made Baby Jacob fractious. He finally fell asleep in Sarah's arms. Jane lifted him carefully into his cradle before going back to her spindle.

"'Tis good to hear the smithy at work again," she said. "Do you know the name of the new man?"

"Edward spoke to him earlier. His name is Thomas Jackson. His father is blacksmith at East Markham."

"Have you seen him?"

"No," said Sarah. "But Edward said he is more than twenty years of age and a strong-looking fellow."

"'Tis good to have a newcomer to the village. He will bring us tales of places we do not know."

"I shall ask Edward to invite him to come and sit with us," said Sarah. "He may welcome the distraction from poor Henry's illness."

"'Tis getting late. Shall I do the milking?" Jane asked.

"Aye. They seem to prefer your gentle touch," her cousin replied.

Jane picked up the milking pail and walked over to the goat shed. The two nannies gave the family sufficient milk for their own use, with a little left over to sell or exchange with neighbours for other necessities.

"I will take some of this to the forge," Jane said, straining the milk through a piece of cloth. They had got into the custom of taking a little milk over to Henry each day in the hope that it would improve his health.

As Jane neared the forge she could see that the doors were open and the embers of the fire were glowing red. A young man was sweeping the floor, his work apparently finished for the day.

He looked up as Jane approached.

"Good day, sir," she said, smiling and bobbing a brief curtsey.

"Good day Miss. 'Tis a glorious evening." He smiled back at her, bowing slightly.

"I have brought some milk for Master Henry. I hope it may do him some good."

"I will take it to him. I have no more to do here today. Who shall I say brought it for him?"

"Jane Walker. I'm the cousin of Sarah Miller." She pointed back the way she had come. "I live at their house, hers and Edward Miller's. He's the local carter." She realised she was talking too much and too quickly.

She handed him the jug and straightened her coif, completely unaware that the sunlight shining on the white linen against her fair hair gave her the look of an angel. She smoothed her hands over her apron, suddenly feeling self-conscious under Thomas's steady gaze.

He nodded. "I had better take it to him."

She watched him walk towards the smithy cottage. He seemed very self-assured for such a young man, and so tall and well-built. She was still standing there when he turned to go into the cottage garden. He looked back at her, grinned and waved. She waved back, blushed deeply and ran back home.

Jane spent the evening spinning, her mind replaying her encounter with the new blacksmith. She hummed to herself, oblivious to Sarah's curious glances towards her. As the light began to fade she set her spindle aside.

"Do I have your permission to go to my bed, cousin?" she asked Sarah.

"Of course, my dear. Sleep well."

She had just got upstairs when she heard men shouting outside and a loud banging on the door. Edward told them to hold their peace as he slid the bolt back, the door crashing open as the men pushed their way into the house.

"Edward Miller, you are accused of rebelling against the King and the Church. You are to come with us. You would do well not to resist for we bear arms."

Jane heard the men leave the house. She looked out of the upstairs window and saw Edward being led away by the men, his hands tied behind his back.

Jane rushed downstairs and closed and re-bolted the door. Sarah, tears streaming down her face, was trying to calm the baby.

"They have taken Edward, Jane."

"Who has? Why?"

"They know we are of the Scrooby congregation. They want to question him. I fear it will not go well for him."

Jane knelt at Sarah's side and put her arms around her and the baby.

"Come, Sarah. We must pray for Edward's safe deliverance."

***

The days passed quickly for Thomas. Word had spread that the smithy was open for business again and he now had work enough for several weeks. He was completing the repair of a harness for Edward Miller. He had not seen Edward for more than two days and, when Jane had brought the milk for Henry, she had said only that he was away. She had seemed unusually subdued and he thought she might have been crying.

"Good day, Master Thomas. How do you fare this day?"

Thomas looked up to see Edward approaching the smithy, a small jug in his hand. He was pleased and relieved to see him but surprised how disappointed he felt that it was not Jane bringing the milk this time.

"Good morrow, Sir. You have come at a fortuitous time." Thomas picked up the repaired harness and handed it to Edward.

"My thanks." Edward looked up from his examination of the repair. "'Tis done well. What do I owe you?"

"Nought, sir. Take it in exchange for the milk."

"I am indebted to you, Master Thomas."

"I hear you have been away," said Thomas. "I hope your business was successful."

Edward's expression darkened.

"'Twas not a matter of choice, my friend. 'Tis perhaps better you have no knowledge of these things for even that may cause you trouble."

"Sir, I did not mean to pry." Thomas was afraid he might have offended Edward.

"No matter." Edward smiled. "Perhaps you will come and sit with us for a while this evening. My wife likes to pass the time in conversation."

Thomas's spirits rose; it would be a pleasant way to pass an evening, particularly if Jane would be there.

Edward was carrying chairs out of the cottage as Thomas arrived.

"'Tis too fine an evening to tarry indoors," he called as he saw Thomas approaching. "'Tis indeed the best part of the day."

"May I help?" asked Thomas.

"'Tis done now. Will you take some ale?"

Edward disappeared into the cottage. Thomas sat down on one of the chairs and surveyed the scene. The garden was abundant with vegetables, soft fruit and herbs. There were fruit trees in a small orchard and bees were flying to and from their straw skeps.

He could hear the baby crying inside the cottage and someone singing a lullaby. Was it Jane? He realised how impatient he was to see her again.

"Good evening, Master Thomas."

He turned to see Jane carrying a cup of ale towards him. He stood and made a slight bow in response to her curtsey. She sat down on the log-chopping stump at his side. Her skin had been touched by the sun and her complexion seemed to glow with health. She was smiling shyly at him, her eyes twinkling with joy and happiness. Thomas gripped his cup of ale with both hands; he did not trust himself not to reach out to take her hand.

"How has your work been this week?" Jane asked. "By all the hammering we have heard, you have been kept busy!"

"Indeed. I hope such demand may continue." Thomas took a mouthful of ale. "Are you not drinking?"

Jane shook her head. "Not at present. I may take some later."

Thomas was starting to feel foolish. Tongue-tied and suddenly shy, he watched as Jane twisted a stray strand of blonde hair in her fingers.

"What is this?" Edward said, seating himself on the chair next to Thomas. "Have you two nothing to say to each other?"

"Nay, Edward. Do not embarrass them!" Sarah was laughing. "Now, Master Thomas, tell us about your journeying. Where did your work take you?"

Relieved to have something to talk about, Thomas began telling them about his travels. Having finished his apprenticeship, he had been on the road for almost two years, seeking work as a journeyman and expanding his skills wherever he could. He had learnt much and had relished the freedom but now he wanted somewhere to settle down. Maybe this was the place.

***

There was a new freshness in the air when Jane followed Sarah and Edward along the lane to Scrooby two days later. Jacob was wrapped tightly against Sarah's chest, fast asleep. They made this journey every Sunday. When she first came to live with her cousin, Jane did not understand their reluctance to attend their own village church in Sutton. Scrooby was quite a distance in bad weather.

They hadn't forced her to go with them but had suggested she should try the meetings at Scrooby Manor for a while. Pastor Robinson and his congregation had made her very welcome. She had found the services refreshingly uncomplicated; there was none of the pomp and splendour of the Anglican Church. Sarah and Edward had said they felt closer to God and she thought she could understand what they meant.

Jane also knew they were breaking the law. Edward's arrest a few nights ago had frightened her and she had hoped that it might discourage Edward and Sarah from pursuing their nonconformist religious beliefs. Luckily he had been released within days. She had overheard him telling Sarah that he had been freed because the authorities had already got the information they wanted from elsewhere. Edward had explained that there were always people prepared to betray others for a small favour or reward, but, if anything, Edward's arrest seemed to have made him even more ardent in his beliefs.

It was early afternoon when they returned from Scrooby. As Jane was setting out their simple meal Thomas rushed in through the open door, obviously alarmed.

"'Tis Henry. He is very unwell."

Jane and Edward ran across to the smithy cottage with Thomas. Henry was sprawled over the table, his eyes closed and his head on his arms.

"I thought he was asleep and I tried to rouse him," said Thomas. "But I fear he may be dead."

Edward wasn't surprised. Henry had been very ill for months. "'Tis God's will," he said, "and a mercy for Henry. God rest his soul."

***

"Good morrow, my friend," Edward greeted Thomas as they passed in the lane a few days later. "How do you do?"

Thomas shrugged. He had not known Henry for very long but he had grown to admire and respect the old man's courage and stoicism. At the burial the previous day it had been clear that his admiration for the old man had been shared by the whole village.

"'Tis time to re-open the smithy," he said. "The rent is due shortly and I have not yet the means to pay it."

The fire in the forge had gone out days ago. It was too late in the day to light one now. Thomas busied himself with clearing the ashes and then sorting and tidying. Henry had accumulated much over the years and some of the items could be refurbished or repaired and then sold. He felt his spirits rise a little; maybe he would be able to find the money for the rent after all.

He looked up as a young man strolled into the smithy.

"Good day to you, sir," said Thomas. He recognised the man; he'd seen him on his first journey to Sutton. It was less than two weeks since but seemed a lifetime ago. "How may I be of service to you?"

"My name is Boothby, Pelham Boothby. I am here on behalf of Squire Vane."

"Indeed, sir. I am Thomas Jackson. I have been working the smithy with Master Redmann. It vexes me to tell you that he went to meet his maker on Sunday last."

"I had heard, Master Jackson. The Squire has instructed me to tell you that the smithy and the cottage must be vacated before the end of the week."

"But why, sir?"

"The Squire has other plans for this site, Master Jackson. I shall come hereabouts on Monday of next week to check that you have vacated the premises."

He untied his horse, mounted and kicked the unfortunate creature into a trot. Thomas watched him ride off, not noticing that Jane was standing only yards away.

"Oh, Thomas. I am so sorry."

"How much did you hear?" asked Thomas.

"Only that you have to leave by Sunday. Do you know why the Squire will not let you stay?"

"I know not. I need to talk to the Squire myself. Perchance I may persuade him to change his mind."

Jane nodded in agreement and watched him until he had walked out of sight.

***

"Thomas is gone to see the Squire and try to persuade him to change his mind." Jane paused for breath. She had rushed back to Sarah to tell her about Pelham Boothby's visit and Thomas's eviction from the smithy.

Sarah pulled Jane towards her in a hug. She could see her cousin was close to tears.

"Perhaps 'tis for the best, Jane. You are become quite fond of Master Thomas and I fear you will find it hard when the time comes to bid him farewell."

Jane pulled away from Sarah's arms.

"What do you mean, cousin?"

"The date for our journey to Holland is decided. A ship will take us from Boston and we will travel to meet it. We leave next week, Jane."

"But 'tis too soon. Why have you not told me afore now?"

"'Tis only just decided and we must be very careful not to tell anyone who may betray us."

Jane nodded. It was illegal to leave the country without permission. There could be serious consequences if their plans were discovered by the authorities.

The feeling of excitement she had experienced when Sarah and Edward had first suggested going to Holland with them had turned to one of anxiety and dread. She knew that living on her own was unthinkable, but she had come to love her life in Sutton and had thought everything perfect. When Thomas had arrived in the village she felt that it had somehow been pre-ordained and had started to believe that destiny would allow them to be together. It seemed she had been wrong.

Jane tried to concentrate on her spinning but the wool kept breaking as her mind wandered. After a while she gave up and went outside to find Sarah.

"Are there jobs for me to do, cousin?" she asked.

"You can sweep the floor and lay down some new rushes."

Jane busied herself with a broom. The fragrance of the herbs laid last time still lingered. Sarah was very house-proud and liked the old rushes and herbs swept out before the new were laid down. Jane wondered how Thomas was getting on with the Squire. If Thomas was forced to leave the village at the end of the week she would have no need to tell him of her family's travel plans. But, if he managed to persuade the Squire to let him stay, she would have to tell him. Even though Edward and Sarah wanted it kept a secret, Thomas deserved to know. She could not just disappear from his life without telling him why.

***

"Good day to you, young master." An imperious voice broke into Thomas's thoughts. He'd been sitting on a fallen tree outside the manor house and had not heard the Squire approaching.

"Good day, Squire." Thomas took off his hat and inclined his head. "Might I beg the favour of a few moments of your time?"

Thomas explained briefly who he was and his interest in the forge at Sutton.

". . . but I believe, Sir, that you have other plans for the smithy," he concluded.

The Squire pursed his lips. "There have been suggestions to that effect," he said.

Thomas detected some uncertainty in the man's tone. He spoke boldly: "Sir, 'tis my belief that I could make the smithy far more profitable than it has been. There is but one other smithy hereabouts and there is much demand for blacksmithing."

"Why is this matter of such great importance to you, Master Thomas?"

Thomas told the Squire how rapidly business had built up in the smithy since it had reopened and his plans for expanding the business by selling refurbished tools at market. He spoke about his wish to settle in Sutton, to marry and have a family. The Squire listened without interrupting him.

"If I let you have the forge tenancy the rent will have to rise. I let old Henry off with a peppercorn rent but you must make it pay. And there will be a fine for the new tenancy."

Thomas had forgotten that he would have to pay to take over the tenancy.

"Yes, Squire. I am content to pay the fair amount."

"There is something else I require of you, young man. If I let you have the tenancy I shall require you to be my eyes and ears in the village. I shall want to know everything that happens, who does not attend the church and most especially whether there are any religious dissenters taking refuge in Sutton. What say you, Master Thomas?"

Thomas felt relief flood through him. He would not have to leave the smithy. He was not happy about being obliged to inform on his fellow villagers but, if he passed only the occasional bit of harmless gossip to the Squire, that may keep him happy. He certainly had no intention of telling the Squire anything significant; not that he knew anything anyway.

***

Jane was back at her spindle. She was certain that the Squire would not change his mind and that Thomas would have to leave the smithy. The wool snapped again.

"May I retire to my bed, cousin?" she asked Sarah.

"Of course, my dear."

There was a knock at the door.

"I'll see who that is," said Jane. She opened the door. Thomas was beaming at her.

"I bring good news," he said. Jane opened the door wider to allow him into the cottage. "The Squire will put up the rent but he will let me stay."

"You have done well to persuade him," said Sarah. "Come and sit with us a moment. Will you take some ale?"

"Thank you. I am parched."

Jane handed the ale to Thomas. Her mind was in turmoil. She was pleased for him that he had secured the tenancy of the smithy but now she would have to tell him about their plans to leave the country, even though Edward had specifically forbidden her to tell anyone.

"Thou art very quiet, Jane," said Edward. "'Tis wonderful news, is it not?"

"'Tis indeed, cousin. Forgive me, Master Thomas. I was just about to retire for the night. My head ails me."

She curtseyed and walked past him to the stairs. Thomas watched her go, a bewildered look on his face.

"I will bid you all good night," he said, walking dejectedly towards the door.

**

The next day, it was well into the afternoon before Thomas took a break. He knew he would have to work hard in order to pay the money that the Squire was demanding. It was not a problem for him; he relished hard work and more jobs were coming into the forge every day. He sat down in the shade at the side of the smithy, took a swig of ale and bit into some bread and cheese.

"Thomas?" Jane's voice interrupted his thoughts.

"Here," he shouted. Jane poked her head round the corner. "This is my hiding place, when I want a bit of peace."

"Forgive me," she said. "I will give you peace."

"No. Come back. I did not mean peace from you. 'Tis good to see you. How is your head?"

"'Tis well, thank you." She sat down on the ground a few feet away from him. He was disappointed that she hadn't come closer.

"Thomas, I have something I must tell you." She paused, clearly distressed. "You must promise not to tell another soul."

He nodded, trying to forget the Squire's condition for granting him the tenancy of the smithy.

"We are leaving, next week. All of us. Forever."

Thomas was speechless, a look of horror on his face.

"No-one here knows. 'Tis something arranged with the Scrooby congregation. The church gives them no peace and 'twill be better for them, for us, to go to another country where we can worship according to our own beliefs." Jane bit her lip. She had already told Thomas more than she intended to.

"Where will you go?"

"Holland. There are others of like mind thereabouts. A boat will take us from Boston." She dabbed at her eyes with a corner of her apron. "I am vexed to be leaving this place, but 'tis the wish of my family."

They sat in silence for a few more minutes, neither of them realising that Pelham Boothby had heard every word. He crept quietly away. He would come back to speak with Master Thomas later.

Thomas went straight back to work after Jane had left. He needed to keep his mind occupied. In less than twenty-four hours he'd gone from disappointment to elation and back again to disappointment. It was devastating news.

"Good day, Master Blacksmith."

Thomas looked up. It was Pelham Boothby, astride his horse.

"Good day, Master Boothby." Thomas took a few steps towards the doorway.

"I happened to be passing this way – a courtesy call, if you will. You must be feeling very pleased with the outcome of your visit to the Squire."

Thomas said nothing. The young man's tone offended him.

"The Squire is most pleased with the price he agreed with you. Mind, the rent is just a trifle compared with the value of the information he will get from you." He laughed, dug his heels into the horse's side and yanked on the reins to turn away.

Thomas returned to his work but he was troubled. Was it just coincidence that Pelham had reminded him of his pledge to the Squire so short a time after Jane had given him her news?

He knew that even if he earned enough to pay the rent, the Squire might evict him if he did not provide him with the information he wanted concerning the village. But he would not give information on his fellow villagers to the Squire, not even if it meant losing the forge. There was nothing that would induce him to betray his friends.

***

"Jane, a word."

They were walking back from the Separatists' service at Scrooby Manor. Jane was surprised at Edward's peremptory tone.

"Yes, cousin. You have a worrisome look."

"You must not see Master Thomas again. 'Tis not fair to give him knowledge of our going. 'Twill not go well for him if the authorities suspect that he has sympathies with our cause."

Jane nodded. She could not bring herself to tell Edward that Thomas already knew.

"A wagon will come tomorrow to collect the chattels we shall take. We shall have to carry our bundles with us but we shall be better off than some."

"Can we not travel in the wagon?" asked Jane.

"'Tis too dangerous. We cannot travel on the open trails for fear of being seen. We must take the rough tracks across the fields."

"What will happen to your business?" Jane asked. She knew how hard Edward had worked to build up his reputation.

"My brother has bought it from me. His son will take it over. He and his new bride will move into the house next week."

Jane hoped Edward had received a good price but she suspected that his kind nature would not allow him to profit from his own family.

***

Two days later Thomas was knocking on Edward's door. It was still early and there was a cool autumnal mist shrouding the village. He knocked again; he was sure someone would be up and about. He'd run out of bread and had hoped to get some from Sarah to tide him over.

It seemed strangely quiet. He tried the latch. The door was unlocked. He went inside. Everything was clean and tidy. It was as though they had just gone out for the day, but he knew they had left for good.

He had scarcely seen Jane since she told him of their plans. Until then he had seen her almost every day since coming to the village. He felt empty inside; a huge sense of loss enveloped him. He turned, closed the door behind him and made his way slowly back to the forge.

He shivered. The change in the weather seemed to mirror the change in his circumstances: the warmth of the last few weeks had given way to a dank and miserable haze that hung oppressively over everything.

***

Jane had never felt so tired in her life. They had walked for many miles, avoiding any villages, not wanting to attract curious attention, as they made their way towards Boston.

Every step was taking her further away from Thomas. Edward and Sarah were being very kind to her and she was trying to put on a brave face. Inside, though, she ached to be back in Sutton, with Thomas.

"Shall I take the baby for a while?" Jane asked as she ran a few steps to catch up with Sarah and Edward.

"Ssh." Edward put his finger to his lips. Jane could hear nothing, but Edward, his arm around Sarah's shoulders, beckoned her into the wood at the side of the road.

"What . . .?" Jane began.

Edward shook his head and put his finger to his lips again. They crouched down amongst the undergrowth. Within seconds Jane heard the sound of horses approaching from the direction they themselves had come.

"I cannot see them now," one of the horsemen said. "God's wounds! Pray do not tell me they have escaped us."

"'Tis my belief they have hidden themselves," his companion replied. "'Tis likely they heard our approach. Come, let us search in the woods. They cannot have gone far."

Jane watched as the men led their horses deeper into the woods. Her heart was pounding. As the sound of the horses' hooves faded, silence descended once again. She kept very still, hoping the baby in Sarah's arms would not cry.

It seemed an age before she saw Edward emerge from a clump of trees, followed by Sarah holding the still-sleeping baby.

"Come, Jane," said Edward. "We must take a different route. 'Twill take us longer but, God willing, we will arrive safely at our destination."

"Who were those men?" Jane asked.

"I know not, but I do not doubt that 'twas us they were seeking."

"What will happen if they catch us?"

"Do not trouble yourself with such matters, Jane." Edward's tone was resigned. "God's will must prevail."

That night they tried to sleep under hedgerows. The mist came down and dampened everything. There was nothing to gain by delaying so they started off again before dawn. Jane trudged on determined not to complain about her lot. She kept trying to remind herself of the pilgrims of old who had travelled hundreds of miles to visit shrines and holy places. She was not sure she was devout enough to cope with the privations of pilgrimage.

Edward had hoped they would be within a few miles of Boston by nightfall, but their detour had added some distance to their journey. Nevertheless, tomorrow, if all went to plan, they would meet up with the folk from Scrooby, ready to board the ship.

She wondered what Thomas might be doing now: working the bellows, maybe, trying to get the fire hot enough to soften the metal. She smiled to herself, thinking of his strength, his reliability, his gentle concern towards her. The tears came again.

The mist was thickening when they came upon the farm. Edward knew another night in the open would not be good for Sarah or the baby.

"I will ask the farmer if we can bed down in his barn for the night," he told them as he set off towards the farmhouse.

"Is it safe, cousin? How can we be sure he will not betray us?"

"We must trust in God, cousin. Now, wait here with Sarah."

He was soon back.

"I have paid the farmer a few pence and he will provide bread, cheese and ale for us and allow us to sleep in the barn. Come. At least we shall have some sleep this night."

The promise of a more comfortable night cheered them all. They were so close to boarding the ship and setting sail for their new life in Holland; surely nothing could go wrong now.

They woke at dawn, refreshed from sleep and heartened by the prospect of reaching their destination. They quickly gathered their belongings and set off as the sun rose over the horizon.

Edward led the way for the remaining miles. The ground was boggy and difficult to walk upon but, so near to their goal, they minded little. As they neared the ship, other groups of travellers joined them, people they recognised from the Scrooby congregation. Jane could feel her excitement growing. On the wharf, they handed over most of their belongings to be stowed on board.

"When do we embark?" asked Jane as the light started to fade.

"Shortly, cousin. Be patient." Edward seemed to be trying to sound calm and reassuring but Jane recognised the doubt in Sarah's eyes.

The men came out of nowhere. Armed with pikes and swords, they surrounded the travellers. They were shouting but Jane could not tell what they were saying. Some of the women were screaming, children were crying. Jane and Sarah hugged each other, the baby between them.

"Someone has betrayed us. We must go with them. There is nothing else for it," Edward said.

The armed men searched the travellers, taking from them anything of value. Then they separated the men from the women and children.

"Here, take these," said Edward, thrusting the remainder of his belongings at Jane as he was led away with the other men.

The women and children were being herded away from the wharf as the rain started. They feared they would never see their menfolk again. What would become of them? Things had not gone well for people who had rebelled against the Church in the past.

***

It had been raining continuously for days. The dark clouds and heavy rain made it easy for the man to slip into the forge unseen. He knew Thomas would not be back for some time. The fire was not lit and it took a while for the man's eyes to adjust to the darkness. He picked up the hammer lying on the anvil. It was heavier than he expected but it would make a useful breaking tool. He slammed it into the bricks holding the unlit fire, again and again.

"What are you doing?"

The man turned and looked at the small figure silhouetted against the feeble light from the doorway.

"Get out, lad. Now. I give you fair warning." He raised the hammer.

"No. Stop. You must not do this." The timid voice was anything but threatening but the man wanted no witness to his crime.

As the child moved nearer, the man let out a shout and leapt forward, the hammer raised. He missed his footing as he struck out, but the weapon found its mark.

***

It was little more than a week since Thomas had last seen Jane and she still filled his every thought. He was waiting at the crossroads at Tuxford. He had been told to meet the Squire there at dawn and it was now late morning and still raining. He turned as he heard a horse approaching.

"Good morrow, Master Blacksmith," the Squire called as he approached Thomas. He guided his horse in a full circle around

Thomas before coming to a stop, straightening himself in his saddle and looking disdainfully down at Thomas.

"You have not fulfilled your part of our bargain. What have you to say about that, Master Blacksmith?"

"I know not what you mean, Squire."

"A liar, too, I do declare. You are not the man of principle you did lead me to believe. Are you trying to tell me that you did not know of the carter's plan to depart from Sutton?"

"Sir, the carter told me nothing of his plans."

"And the little wench who is his wife's cousin and who I am told you have a fondness for. What of her?"

"Sir, I have not seen Miss Jane for more than a week."

"You are no more than a rebel yourself if you protect such dissidents, Master Blacksmith. Get gone from my sight. Were you not paying me the highest rent of any of my tenancies I should have you run out of Bassetlaw. But, as you have reneged on our agreement, I shall double your rent forthwith. If you cannot find the means to pay, you may leave. Good day to you, Master."

Thomas watched as the Squire rode off. He had been very fortunate to get the tenancy at the Sutton smithy but paying double the rent to the Squire would barely leave him with enough to live on. He would have to try and find another forge somewhere else and that would not be easy.

***

The rain became even heavier as Thomas neared the forge. He was soaked to the skin and shivering. He would light the fire and start on his work; there was not a moment to lose now that the Squire had doubled his rent.

The door was half open; he was sure he had not left it like that. He went in and surveyed the scene in horror. Everything that had been neatly stacked, ready to be refurbished, lay broken and cast around the floor. The forge had been smashed and the bellows split open. His tools were damaged beyond use. He sat on the floor, his head in his hands. Had the Squire organised this? Wasn't doubling his rent sufficient price for his refusal to betray his friends?

In the gloom, he heard a sound. It was barely audible and Thomas was so immersed in his sorrow that he hardly heard it.

"Who's there?" He listened for a response.

He stood up. It was difficult to see but something was moving near the anvil.

"Who are you?" he asked, moving closer. A small figure was lying on the floor, wearing a smock and breeches that were far too big; his hat fallen across his face.

He picked the boy up and carried him nearer to the doorway where there was more light.

"Thomas, 'tis me."

"Jane! I never thought to see you again. What happened?"

"We were betrayed when we reached Boston. I managed to escape."

"And the clothes?"

"They are Edward's. I thought people would not heed a boy labourer on the fields and the lanes."

"Where is Edward?"

"He was taken prisoner but now he is reunited with Sarah and the baby in Boston. They may try again to leave for Holland."

He carefully stroked the hair back from her forehead, revealing a large, swollen bruise.

"Who did this to you?"

"'Twas Pelham Boothby."

"Could you swear to that?"

"'Twas very dark and without other witnesses I doubt my word would stand against that of a gentleman. But 'twas surely him. I knew his voice."

Thomas was thinking hard. The Squire would not want a public accusation against Pelham. Maybe there was another way to achieve justice.

He helped Jane into the cottage and made her comfortable.

"Wait here. I shall not be too long."

***

Jane woke with a start. Her head ached and she felt sick and disorientated. She tried to remember where she was.

Thomas shut the door quietly behind him. He took a light from the embers of the fire and lit a candle.

"Did I wake you?"

"'Tis no matter. Where have you been?"

"To see the Squire. He is most displeased with Pelham – although I do believe not so much for wrecking the forge, more for allowing himself to be recognised. I told him Pelham was lucky not to be facing a hanging; he could easily have killed you."

"Tis true."

"Pelham will return to his family in Worksop. The Squire has offered to reduce my rent to what Henry was paying him if you will agree to keep silent."

Jane started to speak.

"No, Jane. Hear me out. With a lower rent I can afford to take a wife. Wilt thou wed me?"

Jane did not hesitate for a moment.

"I will, Thomas."

***

Late October 1607

Their wedding day dawned bright and unseasonably warm. Wearing a silk dress borrowed from the wife of Edward's nephew, who had been wed not long before, Jane walked the short distance to the church, surrounded by the unmarried girls of the village. Her excitement and happiness were tempered only by the absence of Sarah and Edward. They had hardly been out of her thoughts since she had left them in Boston.

Most of the villagers were at the nuptials. Jane and Thomas made their vows at the altar and turned to leave the church. The bells were ringing, the sun shining through the open door. Jane could just make out a couple standing in the shadow of the porch. As she and Thomas drew nearer, they could see their mud-splattered and torn clothing. Were they poor people seeking refuge and charity?

"May you both be very happy," said the woman.

"Sarah!" Jane let go of Thomas's arm and flung her arms around her cousin.

"You took my only spare clothes, Jane," said Edward, laughing. "So I could not dress fittingly for your wedding."

They had much to talk about. Without doubt Edward and Sarah would make another attempt to escape to Holland. Next time, though, Jane would not be going with them.

STEVE TAYLOR

HIS BOOTS

Steve Taylor is an English Teacher and the author of several plays and musicals which have been performed across the Midlands. 'Scroogie Spooktacular!' and 'Jimmy Swift' both ran full weeks at Mansfield Theatres.

He was winner of the Tesco Word-craft/ Bassetlaw Short Story competition with 'Little Miss Sunshine'.

As a singer /song writer he had the thrill of hearing his recordings on BBC national radio and in parts of the USA.

His first novel 'Now You See It?' is currently doing the rounds of agents while he continues to work on short stories and two more novels.

An avid reader, he looks forward to all this year's published entries.

HIS BOOTS

Lucio knew they meant to hang him at sunrise. As the next day would be February 29 in the year of our Lord 1344, the monks hoped that his soul would wander four years lost in darkness. However, after the horrors he had witnessed in the tunnel, Lucio knew there was a darkness to be feared which was worse than Death. Much worse.

At the last moment the wheezing guard tugged the sack from his head and booted him down the steps into the gaol cell. His cheek smacked against the damp stone floor, a stinging pain shot through his skull and for the third time that day Lucio lost consciousness.

The gaoler spat on him and heaved shut the heavy door. Having punched his prisoner until his knuckles split and manhandled him across the muddy grassland behind the church he was ready for a pitcher of ale.

Maybe an hour later, with aching limbs Lucio eased himself to a sitting position and tried to adjust his focus to the dingy surroundings. A milky wash of moonlight seeped through the one high and narrow window. He made out scatterings of straw which, from the stench of the place, had been taken from the nearby sheep pens. He knew the Priory sprawled over several acres and from the freezing dampness guessed his location to be somewhere close to the river.

What a contrast to just two days ago when he kissed his wife and baby goodbye and took a chilly cart-ride from his home in Sheffield. There were lacings of snow upon the hedgerows and piled at the sides of the rucked cart tracks. On the road into

Worksop he passed hunched figures pushing hand-carts and a few small children with down-turned mouths who gazed upon him as though he were some exotic creature.

Brother Thomas had welcomed him with open arms. Ushered into the Calefactory, one of the few buildings in which a fire was permitted, Lucio was encouraged to lug off his leather boots and warm his feet by the flames. Thomas brought him a mug of hot ginger and cinnamon.

"Lucio, you are most welcome, and may I thank you for the speed with which you have responded to our urgent request. This is indeed a matter for delicacy and discretion. I have arranged accommodation tonight in the Gatehouse and you may stay as long as you wish."

"My pleasure, Brother Thomas. One of my earliest memories of Worksop was when my father came here on business. At that time the Gatehouse was still under construction."

"Your father was a loyal friend of St Cuthbert's and a brave man to leave his native Italy in pursuit of a better life for his family."

Brother Thomas looked out of the window where a group of monks in black woollen robes were making their way to prayer. Hoods up and heads lowered against the biting wind, hands tucked into sleeves for warmth, they resembled enormous ravens.

"Lucio, may we flatter ourselves that your memory of the Gatehouse building work in some way inspired you to become an expert in Masonry and Construction rather than following your father into the exportation of cloth?"

"Yes. Papa wisely advised against it. And when the Flemish traders came to dominate the trade we lost our large home in Attercliffe. Papa was a broken man and I knew I had made the right decision."

"We were indeed sad to learn of his passing. When you have

warmed your body we will dine."

And what a meal it had been! Joined by Thomas and three others he ate a haunch of venison fresh from Sir William's western estate bordering Clumber Park. The dark succulent meat was islanded on a large platter of root vegetables and served with a bramble sauce and flagons of pear cider.

Two of his fellow diners were taciturn men who smiled but added little to the conversation, which was largely between Brother Thomas, Lucio and the most imposing of that company, Brother Paul, a small hook-nosed man with a powerful fire in his blue eyes.

Advanced in both years and seniority here was one who enjoyed direct access to the Abbot. Others moderated their speech within his hearing and averted their gaze when he approached. Although lacking in physical stature Brother Paul commanded respect and he had the threatening demeanour of one who walks through life sure-footedly and unchallenged.

Indeed, just as Lucio was about to instigate more small-talk, Brother Paul cut in with the edge of his hand and silence fell across the pleasantries.

Despite the log fire and the cider glow on every cheek, the room became icy as the elderly gentleman bowed his head, pinched the bridge of that hooked nose in deep thought and commenced a monologue none dared interrupt.

"Worksop's reputation for producing the finest malt has come at a heavy price for some of our citizens. Plenty here neglect their duty to God and have to be dragged from their meagre dwellings to give thanks to their Saviour. Dragged because they are the inebriated victims of temptation. Without our intervention such souls would be strewn across the battleground in the fight against Evil. We persevere. And yet we are now presented with a most formidable challenge."

He paused. Lucio felt as though each man in that room had ceased to breathe. A log fell in the grate, sending up a shower of sparks and Brother Paul resumed in a grave tone.

"Uncertainty has crept into our little community. A whisper of doubt. A whisper which left unchecked may grow into a scream. And this scream could crack open the foundations of all we stand for. Which is why you sit before us this day. Lucio, the good name of our town may rest in your hands."

Unsure how to react, yet recognising a compliment, Lucio flushed and took a sip of his cider which now tasted flat and sour.

"I am grateful of the chance to perform any service in aid of a town so beloved of my father."

All eyes were on him as Brother Paul continued.

"Over a century ago a tunnel was constructed connecting St Cuthbert's Priory to Worksop Castle, a fine motte-and-bailey affair on Castle Hill. This fortress was demolished and some of its rubble used to seal up the tunnel at the Castle end. The best masonry was used to construct the walls and smaller buildings in our grounds. Over the years further structural weaknesses has led to collapses of the tunnel roof until only a section of about a hundred yards remains accessible from beneath our place of worship. This we use for the cold storage of wine and meat. At shearing time it becomes a Cellarium for wool. Last week two events occurred which sit heavily upon our hearts. A young boy was dispatched down the tunnel on an errand for Brother Thomas. The boy never returned."

The quartet of godly men were scrutinising Lucio, trying to gauge his reaction. Lucio sought the name of this unfortunate child.

"He was a poor mute found on the outskirts of Lincoln by Brother Peter eight years ago. He was some four years of age and wandering perilously close to deep water. There were no nearby settlements from which he might have strayed and the boy clung to Brother Peter's robes, relieved to have found a kindly face. As the shadows of evening were lengthening Peter took pity on the child and brought him to us. In honour of his protector we accorded him the name Peter and nurtured him in the ways of our Lord providing food and education. In return he performed his share of daily tasks such as fetching water, kindling for the few fires we allow and helping in the kitchens. Such a gentle soul locked in his world of silence.

On the day in question he was given a torch and asked to fetch up some apples we had stored away in the autumn. Peter was given the usual warnings not to go beyond the designated area and to stay clear of where the roof had fallen. After half an hour he failed to emerge. Brothers Andrew and Simon lit torches and followed. When they returned it took four men to hold them down and still their quaking bodies. What they reported still haunts my sleep."

Lucio Giusti, now wished he had fled upon hearing what came next. He would have been spared the horrors of his own descent into that ghastly place. He would now be home in Sheffield in his cosy cottage holding his baby daughter. Instead, he lay crumpled in agony in this foetid cell awaiting death, and his discovery in that tunnel would remain forever a secret.

His fingers delicately explored his ribs, which on the left side were tender where the guards had kicked. Agony lanced through his right knee, which was probably dislocated. The beating he received on the way back from their hastily convened court had been brutal.

At that moment a shuffling in the corner of the cell and movement in the gloom set his heart knocking like a sparrow trapped in a box. After his experiences underground any movement on the periphery of his vision was likely to revive terror beyond imagining.

"Sir, please do not be afeared or angry." A thin voice rose from the straw.

A lad some twelve or thirteen years of age emerged. His thin wrists and dark eyes betokened neglect and malnourishment.

"You startled me is all," confessed Lucio, squinting to make out his fellow prisoner. "I was resigned to spending my final hours alone. I am glad to have the company of a Christian soul. By what name are you called? I am Lucio. Come closer and tell me why one so tender in years has been placed in such a desolate hole?"

The boy scratched his unkempt mop of hair, which was revealed in moonlight to be pale as the straw whence he had crawled.

"Sir, I am called by many names in this awful town but my parents did christen me Bartholemew. I am being punished, I suppose, though they have not told me the crime."

After his own treatment Lucio was not surprised that the good brethren of St Cuthbert's could condone the incarceration of a child.

"Why are you here, sir?" asked the boy, moving closer and drawing up his knees for warmth. Lucio noticed that Bartholemew wore only a thin shirt and patched breeches. His ankles were bruised and his bare feet white and dirt-streaked.

"Before I tell you my story I want you to have these," and with a painful effort Lucio took off his leather boots and tossed them over to the boy.

"Sir, I couldn't accept such a gift."

"I am to be hanged at sunrise. When you have heard my tale you will realise that I do not deserve such a fate. The boots will no longer be of use to me. And it is my will that the guard shall not filch them, thus benefitting from my demise. You are cold. Please put them on."

Although much too large, the boy gratefully slipped his feet into the boots, which came right up to his knees. Resting his chin almost on the rim of the boots, he listened. Leaving out no detail as the chill of a February night gripped that malodorous dungeon, Lucio recounted what the fearsome Brother Paul had told him at supper.

How, in pursuit of the missing boy, Brothers Andrew and Simon had ventured to the end of the tunnel where masonry and soil were piled forming a barrier. How they had found by the flickering ochre glow of their torches a gap in the debris near the tunnel roof. The hapless boy must have been tempted to scramble through it to sate his youthful curiosity. How from beyond that hole there issued forth unearthly sounds of groaning, shrieks as of animals in agony and finally organ music so loud it penetrated their bodies making them vomit where they stood offering up hasty prayers. How a rank odour of decay swept through the gap and pursued their flight down the tunnel with a cacophony of swarming horseflies about their ears. Near-sighted Simon was clutching Andrew's hood so tightly that he pulled him back onto the ground where huge horseflies bit their faces. By the time they had regained fresh air both Brothers were delirious with fear.

The boy was gripped by this narrative and shuffled closer. He assured Lucio that he was not afraid.

Rags of cloud slid across the moon's white face and the winter chill seemed intensified by Lucio's words.

Brother Paul had admitted that he initially attributed the monks' reactions to a heightened sense of expectation. As men who lived internalised lives and who were attuned to spiritual vicissitudes he believed they had experienced a shared hallucination including perceived sounds and odours.
There were no marks on their skin to indicate insect bites. He

further maintained that the lost child must have suffered a fatal accident whilst exploring beyond the fallen roof. And now he required a rational man like Lucio, with his expert knowledge of subterranean structures, to descend into that place and verify his theory. The wild assertions of his fellow monks would be disproved and silenced.

As Lucio sucked in a long, painful breath to continue his narrative, the gaol door was flung back and the guard stood framed in the doorway holding a candle at arm's length. The light etched his face to reveal missing teeth, a swollen, pitted nose and grey stubble. There was a bloodied rag tied around his hand.

"Shut your noise, dead man. Some of us are trying to have a few hours' rest," he wheezed. "Sun'll be up soon enough. Then you won't be making any more noise, will ya? You won't be able to go spreading your lies. So shut your mouth. And if you can't I'll come back and kick it shut."

With mumbled curses, he slammed the door and a heavy bolt grated back into place.

The vile creature had ignored Bartholemew, who had retreated to the shadows. Now trembling a little, he shuffled in his new boots to sit once more facing the condemned man.

"Please tell me what happened," urged the boy in a low voice and drawing closer so they could converse without prompting the return of their captor.

"I deemed it wise to agree with Brother Paul that the monks must have imagined the various sounds and smells, so for my part I had no fear of the day ahead. I judged that my work would be quickly concluded. I passed a pleasant evening at the Gatehouse. My room was small, but from the window of the main hall I could gaze down the tree-lined avenue to the church. Frost on the grass and a clear sky seeded with stars made quite a serene picture. The huge Priory was bathed in a blue glow that spoke of nothing but peace. I also felt protected by the statues of St Augustine and St Cuthbert, which adorned the front of the Gatehouse. All was well."

Lucio explained his reputation as a structural engineer: he specialised in treating stone. Sometimes church pillars were constructed of stone, which eventually proved altogether unsuitable. Once it had been allowed time to fully dry, impurities came to the surface. Untreated, these impurities could lead to dangerous weaknesses. He had developed a chemical which fought against these impurities and entered the stone to 'drive away the badness at its heart'.

At least, these were the terms in which he explained it to one so young and unlearned.

"Next morning I dined with Brother Thomas on quails and dandelion root coffee. He talked little. I then had to wait until the mid-morning prayers had been concluded at nine before he could escort me to the tunnel's entrance, which lay beneath the east side of the Priory some six yards from the end of the long nave.

As we approached we scared up a crow, which shrieked like a wounded infant and flew up into the firmament until it was just a burnt rag in the deeps of that grey February sky. At the edge of the old cemetery was a flight of steep steps bordered by brambles and elderflower trees. The air, already cool, became icy as we turned a corner at the foot of these steps to find a heavily chained door of vertical iron bars.

The chains were a recent addition and Thomas removed them with such dexterity that I guessed him to be the progenitor of their existence.

'May God protect you,' he whispered.

After several fumbling attempts occasioned by the shaking of his hands, he ignited the pitch of a torch and handed it to me. His expression was that of a man who hopes for a positive outcome but who is already resigned to hearing the worst.

As I entered that black corridor a putrid essence made me gag. I had to adjust my breathing before I could accustom myself to the stench. After a few yards I saw nothing remarkable: a stack of parcels of wool and rudimentary shelving holding dusty bottles of some alcoholic beverage; next came sides of lamb and flitches of bacon wrapped in cloth. I judged these to be quite fresh and patted the firm flesh. It was somehow reassuringly solid.

After a few minutes I found myself trudging over uneven ground with only the bare tunnel walls for company. I held the flame close to the rough hewn stone. I had to admire the eleventh century architects who had conceived of such a burrow so close to pasture land, two rivers and running originally for a mile beneath the Priory to what must have been a busy castle. Lead was conveyed to the castle from Sheffield for transportation by water to the far corners of England. The emptied carts were then filled with malt for the return journey.

Just as I was musing on the past, a low scraping jolted me back to the present; I attributed the sound to some rodent scuttling along.

A few yards further I came to the blockage where the tunnel had collapsed, and indeed espied the small gap at the apex of this rubble.

It was from this opening that the scraping sound emanated and I speculated the missing child might be injured and trying to extricate himself. After all, Peter was a mute, unable to shout for aid. Careful of my footing, I began to climb the pile of masonry until my shoulders were level with the opening. I concluded that I could easily get through and there seemed to be some ten feet before the drop down to whatever lay on the other side. The arch of the roof appeared intact and unlikely to fall. Holding the torch before me and wary of my predicament should the light be extinguished, I eased myself up and into this opening where, despite my leather coat, jagged stone fragments bruised my sternum and dug into my ribs. The climb down the other side was easier and I found myself in a clear stretch of tunnel with no rubble or damage. The scraping sounds had ceased. I didn't proceed far, however, before I detected the low hum of organ music – muddy and discordant as if played from under water.

And then I saw it.

To my right I detected a deeper blackness within the blackness of the tunnel side. It was a V-shaped fissure tall enough for a man walking upright to enter – a tunnel offshoot from the main tunnel, if you will, but one which was not man-made. Heart racing and blood pounding in my ears, I poked the dim torch into this fissure. It was a wide enough passageway.

I took a few hesitant steps. The ground was unbelievably smooth as if polished and my progress unimpeded. Up ahead seemed to be a dead end until I reached it and to my surprise found myself turning a corner. When I held aloft the torch its light suddenly intensified to a white brilliance and exposed a small cave – a cave where laid before me was the most ghastly scene."

Lucio shook his head and choked back a sob. He made an attempt to stand but the burning pain in his knee was nauseating. He slumped back against the wall and sighed.

"Oh, Bartholemew, it grieves me to assail your innocent ears with what I beheld."

The gaol was now so cold he could see his breath dying in wisps.

"You must," urged the boy." I need to know it all."

"Initially I thought the floor of that tiny cave was glistening with a wealth of fabulous jewels. And then, as if it had been withheld from me, the powerful stench of putrefaction swept into my nostrils and lungs. I wanted to heave out the contents of my stomach, but my horrified eyes remained fixed upon what I now recognised to be a carpet of human flesh. Flaps of skin, fragments of gleaming bone and the grey viscera of intestinal matter were spread in a pool of congealing blood. It was as if Peter had been ground into a thousand scraps. And on the wall above this monstrous spectacle, in large, crooked letters, was one word written in blood: 'PORTA'.

At first I connected this with the child's name. The truth when it hit me was far more devastating. The word was Latin for 'Gateway'. The implications froze me to the spot. I was desperate to flee yet my feet seemed rooted. My treacherous body betrayed me and would not respond. The moan of the organ music swelled and dipped, seeming to taunt me in my helplessness.

And then I became aware that I was not alone.

From a recess to the right of the cavern there emerged a shuffling figure some eight feet or more in height and clad in grey rags of what appeared to be ancient coarse material. Closer inspection revealed the rags to be rippling like flesh as if the garment was composed of living skin. If this creature had a face it was mercifully hidden by a large hood.

It inched towards me and stretched out a hand with long, thin fingers. This became the claw of some terrible bird and then once more a hand. The bony index finger pointed directly at me and the music dissolved into a diabolical chant somewhere in the bowels of that cursed pit. The raucous voices of a thousand maniacs combined in mockery of the sweet songs of our Holy Brethren. All the woes of the world seemed held in their shrieks and lupine howls, and a tremendous sorrow descended upon my heart. I began to weep and as the tears fell I found that I was now free to move. I wanted to crumple to my knees and surrender. The urge to despair was overwhelming. Surely God touched me in that moment of need, for instead of bowing before that dark entity I gathered what was left of my wits and fled.

My palms slapped against the walls as I skidded and slid back to the tunnel.

The chanting grew louder. The same few indiscernible words over and over wormed into my mind, trying to obliterate reason. Lungs blazing with the effort of running, the torch casting haphazard spikes of shadow up the walls, I reached the jumble of masonry.

Throwing the torch before me, I scrambled up into the gap, tearing my fingers on unforgiving rocks. As I was half way through a claw-like hand gripped my calf and begin to pull me. Talons were digging into my muscle. Screaming openly in abject fear, I managed to thrust back the heel of my other boot and felt something slippery give way beneath it."
Hoping Lucio wouldn't notice, the boy stole a nervous glance at the right heel of his new boots.

"I was free. I tumbled down the other side, allowing the dying torch to clatter to the ground.

Instinct propelled me to the exit, where I fainted into the arms of Brother Thomas.

When I awoke it was to the pungent odour of a rag dipped in sal ammoniac waved beneath my nose. I was laid on a bench before the fire in the Calefactory with Brothers Thomas and Paul peering down at me."

Lucio had to breathe deeply to steady his racing pulse: recounting his tale so vividly had left him drained.

Bartholemew looked troubled not just by the horrors he had heard but by the injustice of it all.

"Sir, you had done these Brothers a fine service. You had risked your life to uncover the truth. Why didn't they thank you for such courage and honesty?"

"If only the world were made of decent folk such as you and I," smiled Lucio, patting the boy's smooth cheek, which was damp from tears.

And he explained how those pious gentlemen had recoiled upon hearing gruesome details of the butchery of their boy, yet also exchanged knowing looks and sly nods. Brother Thomas blanched and fell to his knees upon hearing of the word 'Porta' scribed in blood. Brother Paul pursed his lips in anger, leaving Lucio to feel that somehow he was the wrong-doer. Clenching his fist, the little man declared:

"The Abbot must be informed. Sir, you cannot begin to understand the magnitude of the calamity your findings have wrought upon us. It appears that the twelfth century texts are not allegorical cautionary tales but actual testimony."

Lucio recalled his mounting anxiety as they left him and conferred with others in low voices just beyond the door. When they returned, Thomas, still ashen, was bearing a beaker, which contained a sweet amber liquid.

"Mead, valerian and a few other herbs," the frowning Brother Paul explained. "Guaranteed to soothe your mind and fortify your spirit."

Lucio now gave a bitter laugh at how easily he had been duped.

"Bartholemew, I was a fool. This concoction did indeed soothe me for it contained some powerful narcotic. Its effects were immediate and just as in that foul tunnel I was once more powerless to move. Brother Paul leaned in, pushing his hooked nose close to my ear. He spoke in a low confessional tone.

'The forbidden parchments tell of strange occurrences at Worksop Castle some two hundred years past. The Castle had been crucial to our prosperity. What happened there left a stain on our town for generations. At first shadows thickened. Odd sounds were discerned. Foul odours rose from the ground. Men sought rational causes. When none was found, beatings were meted out to the ignorant in an effort to still their tongues. But the horrors multiplied. Grey faceless entities were seen within the Castle walls at night. Children went missing. Hunks of flesh and smears of blood were found in the tunnel. A woeful time. There was no solution other than to demolish that noble edifice and seal up the tunnel.'

I was drifting now, my body heavy and sinking into the bench as if it were a pool of thick cream. I struggled to focus.

'Lucio, we hoped against hope it would not be true. We used you to verify what we already suspected. You see, the tunnel was constructed over one of the legendary Gateways to Hell.'

At this, my heart folded with grief, but my eyes were glass. Numbed by their potion I could not muster a sound.

I had an impression before I totally fell beyond this world that Paul's features softened and he took my hand in both of his. The last words I heard the Holy Brother impart were whispered, yet they echoed around the caverns of my skull.

'Prayer and containment will be our course of action. For the common good these unfortunate episodes must be put to silence. Silence, Lucio. Forgive us.'

And the room spun away.

How deeply I must have slept through all that followed, for the next thing I remember is being roughly shaken back to wakefulness by our gaoler. He slapped me across the face for good measure. I could only make a muffled protest, for a rag had been rudely tied across my mouth. I found myself securely tied to a chair in a small room with heavy crimson drapes and tapestries covering the stone walls. I saw no windows. I guessed it to be late afternoon. Several fat candles illuminated the stony-faced men assembled in what I quickly understood to be a hastily convened courtroom. Brothers Paul and Thomas were seated either side of a white-haired man in a fine brown tunic. His black knee-high boots were of the latest fashion and had many gleaming buckles. He exuded wealth in that place of austerity and clearly carried great weight in this town. His fingers drummed his thigh impatiently as he waited for me to focus.

A few other monks sat with bowed heads to the left of me on a little row of chairs. Around the room were three, maybe four, guards and at my back the gap-toothed buffoon who had struck me. I was to be afforded no chance to speak. As the great man delivered his words Brother Paul just looked me in the eye with no lingering trace of compassion. Brother Thomas folded his hands and prayed in silence.

'I see you are attentive at last. Heed my words for I have little time to waste on such as you. The fantastical things you claim to have experienced as real we refute as wild flights of fancy, such as might be told to children by the hearth in the dead of winter. In this ignorant land there are those who might believe as fact these picturesque yarns you peddle so liberally. And your disturbing tales reflect badly on our peace-loving community.'

I tried to protest and to struggle against my bonds: it was futile.

The important personage ignored my muffled protestations and continued.

'It has been declared by the Abbot himself that you are a dangerous man. To protect the sanctity and reputation of our town your foul lies cannot be allowed to flourish. And what the Abbot decrees we must obey, for obedience is the path to perfection and transgression is not an option. Sir, you are a blasphemer and an instrument of Satan. Your aims are the destruction of Religion and the establishment of chaos and despair. The allegations you make undermine the very principles by which we live. The scaly wings of deceit must be clipped. Therefore I have decided that you will be taken from here to the gaol which lies at the edge of Buselin's meadow, whence at first light tomorrow, February 29, you will be conveyed to the gallows. Built by our beloved Richard de Lovetot and situated at the junction of Kilton and Radford, the gallows have stood as a warning to malfeasants and rarely been used for execution.

Your head will be covered and your hands tied as if in prayer, that with your final breaths you may offer up supplications to Heaven and beg our Lord for redemption. You will be swiftly hanged by the neck until your soul is released from its earthly bonds. We further decree that your body shall not be publicly displayed but that your remains be dismembered and consumed by flames before sunset that same day. No records will exist of your execution.

Your wife will be duly informed of your accidental interment beneath the Priory following a further collapse of the tunnel. Your remains, deemed unreachable, will thus be accorded repose in the sacred underbelly of our place of worship.'

At that, the sack was slipped over my head and I was carried, chair and all, to a corridor where I was beaten about the ribs and knees. They untied me and removed the gag so that I could finally cry out my pains. They left the bag from my head until we had passed the eastern end of the Priory where, by the eerie glow of many torches, I beheld a chain of monks passing stones and wooden struts from hand to hand as they sealed off the entrance.

I pray their efforts will prevent the servants of Evil from crawling out into this world. Having encountered the agents of darkness I suspect those monks working long into the night will merely delay the inevitable. Peter may have been their first victim, maybe not.

But he will certainly not be the last. The venomous tide will seep above ground and one day Worksop will go to Hell."

Lucio paused. A low echoing hum startled him. Only when it became a discernible tune did he realise it must be three a.m. The Augustan brethren were chanting the Lauds.

"Only four hours until sunrise."

Another tear coursed down the pallid cheek of the boy and sparkled like frost at first light. Lucio wiped away the tear and stroked his hair, which felt like ice.

"Bartholemew, please don't be sad for me. I am one who has stared into the very maw of Hell. And my reward for doing the bidding of these respectable men is to be death at the end of a rope. Yet I will stand blameless before our Lord. I need to ask if you will do something for me. If you consent then I go to my maker with a lighter heart."

The boy raised his head and nodded.

"When you are released, I beg you to tell my story to all who will listen. Tell it exactly as I have relayed it to you; that way others will learn of my heinous discovery and my family will come to know of my true fate. Bartholemew, you represent my only hope. You do believe all I have said? Please say that you believe. Please."

"Oh, I do believe. All of it," he replied, his voice cracking with emotion.

"Heaven be praised. You are a light to my spirit in these my final hours. Through you there is now hope that whatever diabolical presences lurk beyond that tunnel may be faced down and driven back into Hell. Oh, thank God I found you in the darkness. For you will give me a voice."

"Thank God you found me in the darkness," echoed the boy. "For you have given me a voice."

And Lucio raised his head to search the boy's face and ascertain what he meant by those remarks.

But the boy was no longer there.

Just his boots.

CLARE EVANS

PRAY FOR THEM

This is the first writing competition I have entered so was thrilled when I found out it would be published. It has inspired me to continue writing and enter further competitions in the future.

I have always loved local history and Bassetlaw Museum gave me the inspiration for my short story. Although fictional I researched real events, artefacts and places to bring 16th Century Retford back to life in an enjoyable, accessible way.

I hope this story will inspire people to visit local heritage sites in North Nottinghamshire and rediscover a rich hidden history that we can all be proud of.

PRAY FOR THEM

Agatha looked down at the lifeless body teaming with sweat and gave it a nudge. Emitting a guttural moan, the skeletal body vibrated with such ferocity the straw mattress below bellowed mouldy dust into the room. The nearby candle flickered, then flashed as it instantaneously consumed the air-borne fuel. The smell of wild garlic permeated the room as a pot of sticky, rancid broth bubbled quietly over the open fire.

It was not the first time she had seen this affliction and she feared it would not be the last. But experience and knowledge of the old ways had shown her the sooner it was tended to the better. High fever, coughing and vomiting were always the first signs, and if she reacted quickly with tincture, salve and potion, then this time the bulbous sores might not appear.

Memories of the sticky summer of 1558 were still raw in her mind as she began to strip away the young man's clothing. The once-bounteous fields of golden succour had withered in the unforgiving sun, and been beaten down by the unforgiving ravages of tumultuous rain in early spring. Proud beasts fell where once they stood, as the stench of desperation spread throughout Redford Town. She knew not what had spared her from the great pestilence. The church had preached that only the righteous would live and that prayers alone would eradicate the demons inside. Yet, as the clergy dropped one by one, they had abandoned their loyal flock in fear, disbanding to cleaner lands not affected by this great plague. It was then that Agatha had concluded it was fortune, not faith that cured a desperate man.

Carefully dowsing each rag in tepid garlic water Agatha began to place each piece meticulously on the young man's torso and brow. His skin, pale as buttermilk and as soft of the underside of a newborn calf, burned with ferocious, unforgiving heat. His dark brown hair was matted with sweat and life, yet his strong, squared jaw suggested a man of noble descent who had no business to be in such a humble abode. She cleaned his hands with unexpected ease. Superfluous mud and grime washed away, revealing the smooth and supple hands of a young child. Never before had she held such a gentle hand in a man. They were usually dry, rough and weather-beaten with ingrained muck, the testimony of a hard day's toil. She took time bathing the fingers on each hand. Taking each digit with great care, she gently moved the cloth up and down, inspecting each groove and print with indulgent fascination. An indentation upon his forefinger and grazing on the knuckle indicated a ring had recently been forcibly removed. Alerted by this fact she began to investigate further.

In her desperation to treat the young man's fever Agatha had not noticed before the quality of the fabrics that had fallen to the floor. The brown leather jerkin and well- fitted green brocade doublet still lay next to the open fire, and, most noticeably, a soft cambric shirt made of the finest weave. On closer inspection, his left flank had begun to turn yellow as a dark purple bruise fought its way through. A red line had developed around the sides of his neck where a heavy chain had been yanked away with great force. She felt in time she should check the man's drawstring bag he had concealed under his cloak, but not just yet. His fever had taken a grip and time was of the essence. She would continue to try and save this man's life if possible. Not just for his sake, but also for her own. It had been over twelve years now since she had lost her family to the Great Plague. No more did she want to hide. The memories of queuing in vain at the Dominie Cross for food needed to be purged from her dreams. Was he a man of great wealth and standing, robbed of his possessions on the way to the city of Nottingham? Perhaps he was an envoy to the Queen and she would be rewarded greatly for her loyalty to the Crown. The rumours and lies about her sorcery would be banished forever. Whoever this man might be, she was certain he was a man of substance and that his unfortunate demise would change her fortune forever.

The man's eyes, still sticky with sleep, twitched as he regained consciousness. He breathed in deeply, expecting to smell the familiar odour of his bedchamber. An unfamiliar aroma of heady, pungent herbs filled his nostrils and he realised this room was foreign to him. As his other senses began to reawaken he felt the weight of a coarse woollen blanket thrown across him. Cocooned and unable to move, his hands grasped the itchy straw mattress beneath. Oh, how his back ached on this uncomfortable bed! His palms slid slowly over the sticky salve on his chest. He flinched. A sharp, stabbing pain in his side restricted any movement. A cold, damp cloth draped over his forehead confined his head. The room was silent and still. In the distance he could hear heavy rain bouncing off the hard surfaces outside. Geese honked and bickered at the downpour as they ran to take cover. In his soporific state he dared not open his eyes. A sudden fear overcame him. Was he laid out and about to be interred? A surge of adrenalin kicked through his body as his eyes opened abruptly. He blinked frantically as a surge of light burned into his dormant pupils and the radiance of sunlight beamed into the room.

It took a few minutes for his eyes to fully focus. They darted back and forth as he tried to fathom out where he was. The room was small, yet homely. Clay jars were positioned carefully along crudely fashioned shelves positioned between vertical timbers. These contrasted with whitewashed walls, which in some places had crumbled and were in need of repair. A long oak bench sat next to a large table, with a large pottery jug. Bunches of dried herbs hung from the rafters and assorted cobwebs clung from the thatched roof. He glanced over towards the embers of a once-blazing fire and wondered how long he had been here. The last thing he remembered was riding his horse towards a safe house in Worksop. With only a few hours of daylight left he would have made it before nightfall. It was then he became conscious of his nakedness. Stripped bare of his clothes, he could not escape this captivity. His attention turned to a basket of damp kindling drying out between two small stools. Beyond was a large wooden chest that was secured by a lock. As he lifted himself up onto his elbows, nausea and dizziness struck him back down. He was too vulnerable to run and too weak to hide. A dull thud from the heavy wooden door alerted him someone was entering. At the mercy of his captives, he began a silent prayer.

Agatha came in through the door, cradling newly chopped logs for the fire. Dipping gently in front of the embers she purposefully dropped them onto the floor. Small sticks and dry leaves were then placed expertly over the embers as she gently blew to coax a flame. Short but stocky in build, she had become accustomed to living alone. Chores which often included more manly work had become second nature to her and she was comfortable in the knowledge she was responsible only for herself. Slinging a log on the fire, she turned towards the figure lying in the corner and realised his delirium had disappeared.

"You awake then?" She moved closer to inspect her young charge, kneeling down next to him. He flinched as she took off the wet rag that lay on his head.

"No need for that. I'm not going to hurt you." She felt his brow with the back of her hand.

"How long have I been here?" he rasped. His mouth was dry and sore and tasted rancid from congestion.

"Well, that's a good question. I would say… ". She hesitated as if to calculate the hours she had sat by his side.

"Around twelve nights since you collapsed at my door and a right state you were in. Delirious with heat and fever, banging and shouting as if the Devil himself was after you. You marched in here and cried 'Lord, please forgive me' and dropped like a demon possessed. I tried to talk to you, sir, but you just talked of unworldly things I could not see. Then your eyes shut so tight I thought you was gone. But still sweat poured out and you felt like fire. I feared pestilence, sir, and could not drag you out, so I nursed you here with what I knew."

His face softened at this revelation.

"Then I must thank you and your kin for this great kindness."

She knowingly smiled at this mistake and was unsure of his reaction when the truth was told. "It was no trouble, sir, but I no longer have family. It is just me. I live here alone."

The young man blushed. He had mixed feelings. Although grateful for the compassion she had given him, being undressed and nursed in such an intimate way by a single woman embarrassed him.

Feeling his discomfort, she introduced herself. "My name is Agatha of Bolham Wood and, sir, you need your rest." She began to move away to maintain his dignity and stopped at the sound of his voice.

"I am Thomas of York and.... I am humbled by your kindness."

She turned and reciprocated the polite formalities.

"It is a pleasure to meet you, Thomas of York." She bowed her head with respect and returned to the mundane chores of the day.

Over the next few days Thomas grew in strength. The broken rib he sustained when falling off his horse had begun to heal. Each day Agatha would give him, at regular intervals, various potions and lotions that she insisted would aid his recovery. She measured the ingredients with great skill and precision, turning the table into an apothecary's store of unusual smells and delights: lichens, herbs and wild garlic for pain, fungi, roots and fauna pulped to pastes. He dared not question this formidable woman's wisdom, as these strange medicines seemed to work. Agatha had washed the sumptuous clothes of the man and had given back his shirt, britches and stockings to wear. She also supplied him with an old woollen tunic for warmth that she had hoarded away many years before. Every day followed the same routine. Early in the morning Agatha would disappear, returning with coarse rye bread and the occasional cheese. Pottage was then prepared in the great metal pot that was suspended over the open fire for the evening meal. In the afternoon she would mysteriously vanish after stoking the fire, reappearing at dusk, laden with mushrooms, wild berries and the occasional fish caught in the nearby River Idle. He often gazed with wonderment at the hardworking, resourceful creature, who, despite misfortune, had embraced all the opportunities that Nature's bounty provided.

It occurred to Thomas that this tired, middle-aged woman, wearing a simple, long, woollen dress, apron and cloth bonnet, had been handsome in her prime. Now weather-beaten with age, her skin had thickened, accentuating lines around her eyes and forehead. Her once lush, black hair was peppered with grey streaks that gave the impression of a magpie waiting to steal, whilst her moss green eyes betrayed a disillusioned soul.

Thomas was grateful for the attention Agatha gave him in his convalescence, but she was very guarded about her own life and did not ask questions of her guest. This had suited him. Day-to-day conversation had consisted of nothing but pleasantries and updates about his health. However, his unoccupied mind began to brood. Her actions and demeanour began to trouble him deeply. He had heard many disturbing tales of single women who conversed with familiars, curdled milk and destroyed crops. Although she had been pleasant to him, he felt this lack of questioning could be an indication she already knew of his plight. Had she heard news in town, pilfered his pockets or conversed with the spirits? Perhaps she enchanted his horse and cast a spell to lure him to her door? Vulnerability and doubt now clouded his reason. He prayed to God for strength and clarity as he began to piece together what had brought him to this: a fugitive at the mercy of God's will.

"You and me needs to talk!" Wide-eyed and anxious, Agatha had stormed into the house. Thomas sat up abruptly on the stool, where he was warming his feet near the newly stoked fire. As he had grown in strength he felt he should placate this strange woman by helping with the chores.

"They found a horse, wandering round the top of Saint Swithun's only a week or so back. Black it was with two saddlebags attached to its back." Her voice now was stern and serious as she towered over Thomas.

"They did not know where it had come from so took it up to the manor with the rector from the church. He was worried, see, that someone might be missing or hurt. Turns out it wasn't theirs, so they looked in the saddlebags." Agatha could see Thomas was looking more and more uncomfortable. His face had turned ashen white as he looked away and gazed down at the floor.

"Inside they found a wooden box, some holy books and a Bible. But not any old Bible, a Bible made out of the finest parchment and leather with beautiful pictures of Jesus and the disciples at the Last Supper, all inscribed in Latin. Then they had a look inside this box. Inside was a small silver chalice and paten and a small glass phial with wine." Thomas's heart began to quicken and his palms moistened as he knew his identity was about to be revealed.

"So they begins to think a holy man has been hurt. So they looks at the other books to find a name. But these other holy books were not the ones the rector was using, but Catholic books from Rome!" Unsure of what the outcome of this conversation would be, Thomas closed his eyes.

"They say there is a Catholic traitor in town ready to turn people against the Queen. Lord Shrewsbury has returned to Worksop Manor and wants this priest found. He wants to question him about the rebels on his estates."

This overreaction made perfect sense to Thomas. The Northern Earls' Rebellion had occurred just a few months before. Although unsuccessful, paranoia was growing that all Catholics were rebels and wanted to depose Queen Elizabeth for Mary Stuart. As Lord Shrewsbury was the newly appointed keeper of the imprisoned Mary, he was particularly sensitive to any talk of rebellion.

Agatha moved closer, knelt down and gently placed her fingers under his chin. Tilting it upward so she could look deep into his eyes, she whispered, "So who are you? A priest or a traitor?"

"I am no traitor to the Queen, my dear lady, only a traitor to God."

Agatha's face softened as she recognised the fear and guilt in the young man's eyes. He reminded her of the son that she had lost many years before. This similarity appeased her heart and she had grown fond of his presence in her home.

"You don't look like a priest. Where are your vestments? What brings you here?"

"My vestments are destroyed; I was given these clothes before I fled from York. The Queen's army was there. They were imprisoning and torturing priests who would not renounce the Catholic Church of Rome. Since then I have ridden from place to place, sometimes in safe houses of people of my faith, other times hiding in barns or makeshift shelters within the forest. I have been travelling for two months now, serving the people of my church where needed. I hear confessions of men who now have to attend English masses, give sacraments to souls too ashamed to pronounce their faith and last rites to the old and impoverished."

Agatha sat back on the stool next to his. Her mind was trying to comprehend the damning information that put not only herself in danger but the young priest. She continued listening, intent on finding the reason why he had sought sanctuary at her door. Gazing into the fire to aid his concentration, he continued his tale.

"The night I came to you is very unclear. I had been travelling on my horse nearby, in the thick of Clumber Forest. I had earlier that day stopped by a stream to wash and take on water. I did not have much to eat and was weary from hunger. I remember eating a stale roll that had been given to me the day before. I had given an old gentleman the last rites on his deathbed; his poor family were so grateful that his sins had been washed away that they gave me their last rolls and cheese in return. I remember I started to feel hot. My temples began to sweat and my hands became wet, making it difficult to hold onto the reins. The world started to turn round and my eyes became heavy. I lay forward, holding the neck as best I could, and must have blacked out, for the next thing I recall is the quickening of his pace and the blackness around me. I can only assume he had been startled, as no sooner than I came round he began to gallop with such fervency that I had no way to calm him. I hung on for as long as I could but my limbs had become weakened from the sickness. Before I knew it I was hurled onto the ground and tumbled into a nearby thicket. I do not know how long I was there. I saw a light in the distance ahead. The last thing I remember is ripping off my crucifix and ring for fear of being discovered…and here I am. A coward and a priest who feared for his own life above his vocation."

There was silence. Agatha stood up slowly and went towards the wooden table and poured two cups of watered beer. Taking her time, she pondered on what to do next. She had taken in this man to restore her battered reputation. Cynics and gossips had looked upon her independent single life with suspicion. They had begun to question why she had rebutted the advances of suitors. They in turn started rumours that she must have a partner of a supernatural nature and the old ways she practised were unholy. So far she had dodged the amateur witch-hunters, as her cures for ailments were invaluable to the people of Redford. The truth of her existence, however, was far bleaker than the fanciful stories they had made up.

Agatha sat and offered Thomas a cup of beer. He gratefully took it as a sign of a truce.

"You are not the only priest to run scared and you will not be the last." Agatha spoke gently. She had gotten to know this young man as a person and not a representative of God who was to be revered or judged.

"Many years ago I had a husband, son and daughter who I loved with all my heart. My husband was a baker by trade and we lived in the town. We worked hard every day and were well respected by all who lived there. On market days we would sell our wares to all who would buy in the square. It was a hard but happy life…"

Agatha closed her eyes and smiled as she remembered the warmth of her husband's embrace and the children's laughter.

"Then came a bad time. Crops had failed and a great pestilence befell the land. No one knew why and people began to fall sick. Our house was one of the first that was ravaged by the Great Fever. My children got sick and a giant cross was painted on our door. People were afraid and as it spread quickly throughout the town many thought it was the bread we supplied that had gotten people sick. The priests in the church were preaching that demons had come to the land and were killing the unworthy. So they thought we were putting demons inside our dough."

Thomas looked up into Agatha's glazed, watery eyes. He could see that this painful accusation was not true and he felt ashamed for ever doubting that it might be so. She composed herself and continued.

"The morning my children died a great crowd gathered outside with the priest. He told us we must leave and not return. We gathered all we could and put it on the old bread cart and were marched out of town. They wrapped and slung the bodies of my children into a large pit not far from here. I try to keep them close along with the other poor souls who died."

There was a minute's silence. As a young man Thomas had seen this Great Plague take hold over the land. He knew of the devastation and the lives it had destroyed. None close to him had died. He believed that his Catholic faith had spared his family and this had spurred him on to become ordained. He would be protected by God from the furies of Nature.

"But what of your husband? What happened to him?"

"He died not soon after we came to this place. I nursed him the best I could but to no avail. Every time I pass the Broadstone at Dominie Cross I can still smell the stench of coins dipped in vinegar. The hours I spent waiting for supplies from the sparse market stalls! The priests left without warning and the gentry abandoned their tenants. With no spiritual guidance or structure, people lost all hope. They coped as best as they could whilst grieving for the town they once knew."

Thomas now realised what Agatha meant about priests running scared. It explained why she had not judged him harshly about hiding his true identity.

"Of course, things got better over time. The priests who had fled returned to their flock and began to rebuild their shattered community. People chose to forget the injustice and pain that they inflicted upon them. They went on with their day-to-day lives as if nothing had happened, spurred on by the sermons that God had spared the righteous and that they must give thanks. But what God would abandon his children at such a time of need? Innocents died without proper burial, cast aside with no prayers or thoughts for their souls. I tell you this: I will never forget how my family was cast out and lost all that was ours, and how fear was masked by the religious teachings of man. I am no demon or devil wishing ill on my neighbours, just a widow woman who grieves for the loss of all she once knew."

This outburst of emotion unsettled Thomas. He was not sure how he should respond. It was clear that the clergy had blackened her character and that this injustice did not bode well in his plight. He tentatively spoke from his heart.

"I am so sorry for your loss. I will pray for their souls."

Agatha looked at the vulnerable figure beside her. He was only young and she could sense he was disturbed by the uncomfortable truth she had bestowed on him. It was not intended to frighten him, but a warning of the power clerics had over other people's lives.

"'Tis not your fault. 'Twas a long time ago."

Agatha got up and went to the old wooden chest in the corner of the room. She reached down below her apron and pulled out an old metal key that was suspended on a thin piece of twine. Thomas watched as she placed the key in the tarnished lock and opened it. With some force she lifted the large, heavy lid and peered inside. Remnants of her past life lay before her: a pair of small woollen britches, her daughter's little corn doll and a large wooden ladle used to measure yeast for the dough. Beneath, wrapped in unused clothes, was a set of pewter tableware. On top was the cloth string bag Thomas had hidden under his cloak. It was this that now claimed her attention. She carefully lifted it out and placed it on the table.

"I thought that had been lost!"

Thomas stood up and went towards the simple cloth bag. It still looked full of his belongings. He was surprised his items looked still intact and had not been pilfered by the woman.

"I kept it safe for you."

She stepped back as he started to examine the contents. Inside, neatly folded, were the bare necessities he needed to serve his ministry: a golden chalice with a chasuble, stole, maniple, veil and burse, all intricately embroidered in gold and deep crimson red. Agatha stood aghast as she had never seen such workmanship on any garment before. Only the Queen and royalty were permitted to wear such bold and sumptuous colours. As he carefully laid each piece on the table she began to look at this young man in a different light. Trapped in a power struggle between belief, religion and politics, he did not appear to be the kind of man who would be involved in a traitorous rebellion. One thing, however, she knew for certain: it would not be long before Lord Shrewsbury's men would be knocking at her door, demanding to search her home.

"You need to leave, but first there is something I need you to do…"

At first Thomas had been taken aback by Agatha's request as he felt unworthy of such a task. Many nights he had struggled with his conscience for fleeing from York, when so many of his brethren had stayed and suffered greatly for their faith. He had taken solace in ministering to men, stronger than himself, throughout Nottinghamshire, believing that at least he had played some small part in saving their souls. His greatest betrayal, though, was the night he had denied his faith entirely by ripping off the golden crucifix and ecclesiastical ring in fear of being discovered as a Catholic priest. For this he felt deeply ashamed and daily said penance to expurgate his soul.

The next day, Agatha collected flowers from the nearby wood. It had been a mild winter. Snowdrops and the first wild daffodils were in abundance. Carefully she created three small posies and tied them with some old twine. It had been something she had done for many years, but this year would be special. This year, the remains of her beautiful family would at last be blessed and their souls would be reunited. She knew it would be dangerous for the young stranger to complete this task in the daylight, so it was agreed that on the day of his departure this blessing would be made at dusk. That time of the day had always been special to her. She often looked towards the golden haze on the horizon and half-closed her eyes. Sometimes shadowy silhouettes of spirits would appear in the trees, dancing to the rhythm of nature's breeze. She had always felt one with Mother Earth. Her grandmother had taught her all she knew about the plants that would heal and protect, and how to read animals and the clouds in the sky. She missed these times of innocence, before the harsh truths of adulthood had prevailed.

"Have you got everything ready?" Agatha was excited. It was like a huge weight had been lifted since Thomas had agreed to do the blessing. Overnight her whole posture had changed. She appeared taller, her face had softened and her moss-green eyes smiled with joy. This would be a new beginning, the closure she craved for, yet had never been offered by the clergy in the town. Thomas had noticed this drastic change and it heartened him to see her like this. He, too, although still in danger, felt this was a part of God's plan for him. By completing this task his previous sins would be forgiven and he would be restored to God's favour.

"Yes, I think I have everything I need…" Thomas looked out of the window. It was almost dusk and soon they would have to walk to the nearby mass grave. He checked his bag one last time and picked up the provisions Agatha had prepared for his journey.

"Wait. You are forgetting something." He turned, and Agatha placed two small objects in his hand. Looking down, he recognised them immediately.

"I went back and searched through the thicket for you." Thomas smiled as he gazed down at the small gold ring and crucifix in his hand. Agatha picked up the ring and gently placed it on his finger.

"I think you should wear them," she said gently. "Never be afraid to be who you truly are."

This affirmation meant a lot to him, but he felt the care he had been given deserved more than just his gratitude.

"Here, I want you to have this. For all you have…"

"Sshh!" Agatha stopped him suddenly. In the distance she could hear horses' hooves getting louder as they trotted towards the house.

"There is no time. You need to hide!"

Desperately Thomas looked around the room as Agatha quickly

went outside. Where on earth could he hide? This house was small and sparse. There were no other conceivable exits. He wrapped his long dark cloak around himself. He needed to think, and think fast.

Agatha tried to compose herself as the figures in the distance became larger and more distinct, five of them in all. Two of them carried long spikes, while a third expertly handled a lance at the rear. The two in front were easier to distinguish: a clergyman and man of nobility. As they neared her door she recognised the gnarled, twisted face of the priest who had banished her many years before. He grimaced in acknowledgement. Pulling up the horses, they stopped. The nobleman began his questioning only a few feet away from the fugitive they wished to capture.

"We are on the lookout for a man, a stranger in these parts, who may have been injured in a fall around two weeks ago. Have you seen or heard of such a man?"

"Why no, sir, I don't see many people in these here woods."

"And you haven't found or seen anything out of the ordinary? Things going missing perhaps?"

"No, sir. I have not much and would have noticed if that had been the case."

The priest snorted in disdain. The nobleman turned round and looked quizzically at him, surprised at his rudeness.

"Have you something to say about this matter, pray tell?"

The priest felt uncomfortable in being questioned in such a condescending way. The nobleman had great authority in this borough, and letting his feelings interrupt the investigation this way needed a justifiable explanation.

"This woman is a miscreant and should not be trusted!"

"Really, and why is this?"

Agatha's heart sank. She knew the scandalous rumours about her were about to be aired.

"This woman for years has lived alone in secret, only coming to town when illness or tragedy strikes. She preys on the sick and afflicted, preaching the maladies they suffer can be cured by her. She brings her ungodly lotions and potions and will hear not of prayer, saying demons are imagined by holy men. But I say the truth is this, she has bewitched the people in Redford town and curses all people who do not succumb to her charms. Why, she was seen only yesterday talking to folk at the edge of town. There is no way she could not have known about the man we seek."

"These are strong words and do put doubt on her character…. If any of her actions or enchantments have caused harm or death in the town she will be punished under the Queen's own witchcraft laws. However, the matter of the stranger is more pressing. Guards, search the house!"

Panicked at this accusation and fear of Thomas being found, Agatha threw herself onto the ground. Kneeling, she pleaded with the nobleman.

"No, sir, the things they say aren't true. False lies. I am a good woman. I help people and do no harm."

The guards dismounted and moved towards the door.

"Please, sir, I speak truth!"

Knowing her appeal would not help her now, she backed up and stood against the door. With arms outstretched she began to shout.

"You cannot go in I tell you. You must go! A great sickness is here and you will be afflicted. You will all die if you enter. The pestilence will strike you down!"

The guards hesitated as they stood before her and looked up for guidance at the nobleman.

"I tell you she lies," the priest sneered. "Is this not proof? She is cursing us all!"

The nobleman nodded at the guards to continue.

Agatha let out a bloodcurdling scream as if possessed, and launched herself at the middle guard and spat in his eye. With one swipe he knocked her flying to the ground. Desperate, she grabbed his ankle as he started to lift the latch. Pulling her head up, she bit deep into the back of his knee. Off-balance and screaming in pain, the guard fell to the floor. At that moment Agatha felt a large, heavy object strike the back of her skull. With the woman unconscious on the ground, the three men entered her home. All was silent except for a rhythmic rapping sound above a makeshift bed. The wind had picked up, and the wooden shutters on the window were open, gently tapping in the breeze. Thomas was nowhere to be seen.

The mad woman started flailing her arms round erratically at the children who mocked her. Holding up the small golden crucifix she had found outside her window many years before, she chanted "Pray for them." She was often seen wandering the forgotten mass graves of people who perished in the Plague, chuntering the same desperate plea. Homeless, she lived at the mercy of others. Her home and possessions had been impounded after she had been imprisoned for witchcraft. However, when no witness came forward to accuse her of causing them harm, she was reluctantly released, the condition being she did not return to Redford, lest they be reminded that prayers alone cannot protect from Nature's wrath.

Exhausted, she collapsed to the floor. The children screamed and ran back excitedly towards the dim, distant lights of Tuxford. It was dusk, her favourite time of day. The red and orange hues burnt into the dark indigo sky, exalting the white enamelled Christ on the illuminated golden cross. This was the witching hour where belief and truth were suspended in time. Half-closing her eyes, she watched the orbs of spirits dancing above the unconsecrated graves and remembered the young priest and the promise that he made: a final blessing that would free her family's trapped souls. She often wondered if he had completed the task, but she could not take the chance. Her frail, weak body, malnourished and crooked with age, gasped. Holding onto the cross tightly in her contorted, twisted fingers, she whispered under her breath, "Pray for them", and was gone.

The curator of Bassetlaw Museum sprayed and carefully wiped the streaks off the glass of the new exhibit. This had been a great find for Retford and would surely encourage more people to visit the locality. She looked down in wonderment at the new display, examined and identified by historians only months before. She stood back and surveyed her handiwork.

'16th Century Crucifix. This is made of gold, decorated with enamel and shows the crucifixion of Christ.Jesus's body was originally enamelled white. On the reverse is a Latin inscription meaning "By your cross, save us, Christ." Near Tuxford'.

Yes, that would do: a short and concise description. After all, the antiquity spoke for itself! Gathering her cleaning materials, she walked towards the door and proudly turned for one last glimpse of her new acquisition. It glistened invitingly below the spotlight. As she switched off the light a chill hit the room, making the hairs on her arms stand up. She hesitated as a breeze of cold air moved past her. Unnerved, she stood still in the blackness and heard a whisper, "Pray for them".